FANCY DANCER

Books by Fern Michaels

Wishes for Christmas
About Face
Perfect Match
A Family Affair
Forget Me Not
The Blossom Sisters
Balancing Act
Tuesday's Child
Betrayal
Southern Comfort
To Taste the Wine
Sins of the Flesh
Sins of Omission
Return to Sender
Mr. and Miss Anonymous
Up Close and Personal
Fool Me Once
Picture Perfect
The Future Scrolls
Kentucky Sunrise
Kentucky Heat
Kentucky Rich
Plain Jane
Charming Lily
What You Wish For
The Guest List
Listen to Your Heart
Celebration
Yesterday
Finders Keepers
Annie's Rainbow
Sara's Song
Vegas Sunrise
Vegas Heat
Vegas Rich
Whitefire
Wish List
Dear Emily
Christmas at Timberwoods

The Sisterhood Novels:

In Plain Sight
Eyes Only
Kiss and Tell
Blindsided
Gotcha!
Home Free
Déjà Vu
Cross Roads
Game Over
Deadly Deals
Vanishing Act
Razor Sharp
Under the Radar
Final Justice
Collateral Damage
Fast Track
Hokus Pokus
Hide and Seek
Free Fall
Lethal Justice
Sweet Revenge
The Jury
Vendetta
Payback
Weekend Warriors

The Men of the
   Sisterhood Novels:
Double Down

The Godmothers Series:

Classified
Breaking News
Deadline
Late Edition
Exclusive
The Scoop

Books by Fern Michaels (Continued):

E-Book Exclusives:

Desperate Measures
Seasons of Her Life
To Have and To Hold
Serendipity
Captive Innocence
Captive Embraces
Captive Passions
Captive Secrets
Captive Splendors
Cinders to Satin
For All Their Lives
Texas Heat
Texas Rich
Texas Fury
Texas Sunrise

Anthologies:

When the Snow Falls
Secret Santa
A Winter Wonderland
I'll Be Home for Christmas
Making Spirits Bright
Holiday Magic
Snow Angels
Silver Bells
Comfort and Joy
Sugar and Spice
Let it Snow
A Gift of Joy
Five Golden Rings
Deck the Halls
Jingle All the Way

FERN MICHAELS

FANCY DANCER

KENSINGTON BOOKS
http://www.kensingtonbooks.com

KENSINGTON BOOKS are published by

Kensington Publishing Corp.
119 West 40th Street
New York, NY 10018

This book is a work of fiction. Names, characters, places, and incidents either are products of the author's imagination or are used fictitiously. Any resemblance to actual events or locales or persons living or dead is entirely coincidental.

All Kensington titles, imprints and distributed lines are available at special quantity discounts for bulk purchases for sales promotion, premiums, fund-raising, educational or institutional use.

Special book excerpts or customized printings can also be created to fit specific needs. For details, write or phone the office of the Kensington Special Sales Manager: Kensington Publishing Corp., 119 West 40th Street, New York, NY, 10018. Attn. Special Sales Department. Phone: 1-800-221-2647.

Kensington and the K logo Reg. U.S. Pat. & TM Off.

Library of Congress Control Number: 2015942261

ISBN-13: 978-0-7582-8496-9
ISBN-10: 0-7582-8496-9
First Kensington Hardcover Edition: October 2015

eISBN-13: 978-1-4201-3019-5
eISBN-10: 1-4201-3019-9
First Kensington Electronic Edition: September 2012

10 9 8 7 6 5 4 3 2

Printed in the United States of America

Dear Readers,

First things first. I am thrilled and delighted that *Fancy Dancer* is being made available in print form. This, I think, is a good time to tell you all that I am digitally challenged. I like to hold a book. I marvel at those of you who have moved beyond my Neanderthal stage. I'm getting there, though, slowly but surely. Having said all of the above, writing *Fancy Dancer* was a first for me in the e-book world. I have to say I liked it.

People always ask me, and I think other writers as well, where we get our ideas from. My answer is pretty mundane. From newspapers, television, friends, something I might have seen at some point and stored away the memory for a time when I search the shelves of my mind for an idea.

My idea for *Fancy Dancer* came to me in a cemetery. Hey, no one was more surprised than me, but it did happen! I had gone out there to take some flowers for those family members who were laid to rest beneath huge old oak trees. It's a pretty place, if cemeteries can be called pretty. It is certainly peaceful and quiet, with little stone benches under the umbrella-like branches and meandering stone paths that lead to old memories that are never forgotten.

On this particular day I was sitting on one of those little stone benches, just staring off into space but still aware that people were walking by and leaving flowers. Mostly older people, I remember thinking. I was also aware of all the colorful flowers in the urns attached to the grave stones. Acres of flowers and stone. Everyone was moving slowly, whispering, perhaps out of respect, I don't know. Then out of the corner of my eye I saw this tall young man, his arms full of white roses. It looked like he'd bought out some flower shop. I watched him because that's what I do; I watch people and try to figure out what makes them who they are. He dropped to his knees and spent quite a bit of time arranging all those roses. I put his age at maybe thirty or so. My daughters would have referred to him as a hunk or smoking hot. He was definitely good looking, that's for sure.

While I was trying not to stare, I still was. He looked in such distress I almost got up and went over to him but I didn't. I watched as he got up and punched at the gravestone with his bare hand. *Ooooh*, that had to hurt. But he acted like he didn't feel a thing. Then he did this little whirly gig dance and bent over and held out his hand. Even from where I was sitting I could see this yellow butterfly settle on the back of his hand. I think everyone in the town of Summerville heard him scream at the top of his lungs, "YESSSSSSS!" I kind of felt like doing the same thing there for a few seconds.

I continued to watch as another man approached. Older, very well dressed, suit, tie, the whole works. Kind of odd, I thought, for a day in July. The young man's happiness was short lived, however. While I couldn't hear the words it was obvious the two were quarreling. There was a lot of hand gesturing. The young man used his hand and arm to the older man to move away. He didn't want him near the stone. *Hmmnnn.*

The older man tried to take the younger one's arm. He shook him off. He pointed to the flowers he'd brought. He was angry, really angry. Then the older man said something and in the blink of an eye, the young guy decked him. He toppled backward and landed pretty hard on his fanny. I remember thinking if I had a brain in my head I would have gotten up and left. Did I? Nope.

The young guy stomped off and the older one got up and went after him. The young man stopped, turned around, his arms outstretched, palms facing the older man. Then he let loose again and I heard him say, and I think everyone walking around heard him say, "You're not my father, you're just a sperm donor." The older man just stood there. I was going to leave then and would have but I watched as the yellow butterfly followed the young guy, all the way to his car. The older man finally moved and walked to his car. A chauffeur driven car.

I waited until both cars were out of sight, and then I ran as fast as I could to see the grave marker. In addition to the woman's name it said:

She Was A Dancer.

I thought my head was going to explode as all kinds of thoughts and scenarios raced through my mind. I couldn't wait to get home so I could write it all down.

And that's how *Fancy Dancer* came about.

I hope you enjoy reading it as much as I enjoyed writing it.

Fern

Prologue

Everyone in the hospital corridor knew he was a boy, but an outsider would have taken him for a young man, perhaps in his midtwenties, because of his height—six four, the breadth of his chest, and his obvious physical fitness. He weighed two hundred and forty pounds. His high-school football coaches called him perfect linebacker material. Until one looked into his eyes and saw the moistness and the vulnerability that he tried so hard to conceal. In truth, Jake St. Cloud had just turned seventeen and would leave for college in only three weeks.

The doctor standing next to him could have auditioned for a role in the old television show *Father Knows Best.* He was kindly looking, with gentle, compassionate eyes, wire-rim glasses, and gray hair, which was thinning at the top. At first glance, he seemed neither tall nor short. One just didn't notice those things. What one noticed was the white coat, the stethoscope, and his mesmerizing eyes. Also, his capable hands. Those capable hands were now on Jake's shoulders. Words would come. Jake waited as he sucked in a deep breath, knowing what those words would be and dreading them.

"Just tell me, Dr. Fischer," Jake said in a choked voice.

"I will, son. But first, do you know where your father is? We've been trying to call him all day. We've left messages everywhere, but there's been no response."

"I don't know. I tried calling him before I came, but his secretary said she didn't know where he was, that he hadn't checked in. Does Mom want to see him?"

"No. She asked only for you. Selma refused the last morphine shot. She said she wanted to be lucid and alert when you got here." The gentle hands were still on Jake's shoulders when Dr. Fischer said, "She doesn't have much time, Jake, so make every second count."

Jake swallowed hard. "What if . . . what if my father doesn't get here . . . in time?" He realized what a stupid question that was and shook his head to clear it. He shook free of the doctor's hand and sprinted down the hallway to Room 412.

"Shouldn't we be there, Dr. Fischer?" the stocky nurse asked.

"Yes, but outside the door. Selma doesn't want the crash cart. She signed all the papers. Right now, all she wants is to see and talk to her son, Jake."

"Should I try to reach Mr. St. Cloud again, Doctor?"

A look of disgust washed over the kindly doctor's face. "I think a dozen calls is sufficient, Nurse Gilligan. The man knows his wife's condition. I certainly didn't mince any words yesterday when I spoke to him. He's not here, by choice."

"Jake is such a fine young man. His mother so doted on him. I never heard a bad word about Jake St. Cloud. Do you remember that article about him that was in the paper when he graduated in the spring? I remember every word because I wished someone would say such wonderful things about my own son."

"I do remember. And every word was true. Selma raised a fine son. Taught him right from wrong. Taught him how to be kind, to help others, how to give and give and give. She said he never ever, not once, asked for a thing. That's the kind of young man he is. And on top of all his civic and charitable duties, he was an honor student, as well as one of the school's best athletes. He turned down five different scholarships so other youngsters could get them. He said he was paying his own way. Tell me, what kind of kid would do something like that?"

"A very special one, Dr. Fischer."

"Exactly."

Dr. Aaron Fischer leaned up against the wall and closed his eyes. Nurse Gilligan watched his lips move and knew he was praying for his patient because there was nothing more he could do for her. She closed her own eyes, her lips moving just as silently as Dr. Fischer's.

Inside the hospital room, Jake St. Cloud pulled a chair closer to the hospital bed and reached for his mother's hand. He squeezed it. "I'm here, Mom," he said quietly.

"I know. Did I take you away from anything at home?"

"No. Mika told me to go and get lost. He said he was paid to do the yard work and didn't need me to do the heavy lifting. He's getting old, Mom; I just wanted to help him. He should retire and play with his grandchildren."

"He's been with us forever, Jake. You can't take his job away from him. He'll know when it's time to leave. I provided for him and his family in my will. Loyalty deserves to be rewarded. Always remember that, Jake."

"I will, Mom, I will. I tried calling Dad but wasn't able to reach him."

"That's a good thing. I don't think I could bear to look at him right now. Your being here is all I need. I asked you to come for a reason. When . . . later . . . when . . . when things are over, you're going to have questions. I want you to hear the answers from me. I wish . . . oh, Jake, I wish so many things, but . . . you always said you wanted to be just like your dad. I

4

never wanted that because he's not who you think he is. Please, promise me you won't . . . you won't follow in his footsteps. And there is one other thing, Jake. You're going to hear things . . . things I would give anything in this world for you not to hear. When and if you do, please don't think too harshly of me. Will you promise me to try, Jake?"

A promise to his dying mother. How could he deny her anything? He couldn't; it was that simple. His brain whirled and twirled as he listened to his mother's strangled words. He wanted to tell her to stop, that he didn't want or need to hear the words, but he couldn't get his tongue to work. And, somewhere in the back of his mind, he knew that his mother wasn't telling him *everything*. He didn't know how he knew that, he just knew it somewhere down deep.

"Your father was never faithful to me, Jake. He had his reasons; I have to be honest about that. Every month, every week there was a new woman. Women he made promises to, promises he never kept. He only married me for my inheritance. I like to think I knew that, and that's why . . . He needed my money to start up his business. I gave it willingly because I thought I was in love. It took awhile for me to realize I wasn't in love at all. The only thing I ever got in return was *you*. That was enough for me. I made my life around you and let your father do what he wanted. My lawyer will be in touch with you . . . later. All my money, my holdings go to you. We set up a trust fund for you. It will see you, your children, and your grandchildren through their lives. I want you to use it wisely. Wisely, Jake. I need you to remember that word. Your promise, one more time."

"I promise, Mom."

"Jake, listen to me. Come closer. I know you have a half brother or sister out there somewhere. I hired detectives, but we could never find out who or where he or she is. Your father covered his tracks very successfully. I know this because I overheard your father on the phone one day with the child's mother. Her name was Sophia. That's all I know. I want you to find him or her and make your sibling's world right—the mother's, too. I don't want you to be alone in the world. I want you to have a sibling. I want you to make it right for them. Later . . . later, you'll understand."

"Mom, are you sure?" Jake whispered in an agonized voice.

"Yes, Jacob, I'm sure."

It had to be true, Jake thought. His mother only called him Jacob when something was important. A brother? Possibly a sister? How could that be? "I promise, Mom."

"Good. Now be a good boy and find Dr. Fischer. Tell him I'm ready for my shot."

"Okay, Mom. I'll be right back."

Jake thrust open the door and was halfway down the hall in search of the doctor when he realized that Dr. Fischer had been standing right outside the room. Tears rolling down his cheeks, Jake ran back the way he'd come.

Dr. Fischer wrapped his arms around the boy and led him away from the room. "Your mother is sleeping now. Nurse Gilligan will stay with her. Let me buy you a cup of coffee, Jake."

Across the table in the cafeteria, Dr. Aaron Fischer looked at the young man sitting across from him. Just thirty minutes ago, he'd sent a young boy into his patient's room. The boy sitting across from him had cold, unforgiving eyes; he simply was not the same person who'd entered the room, then left it. The kindly doctor couldn't help but wonder what it was Selma St. Cloud had said to her son. He wondered if he'd ever know.

Jake's hands were rock steady around the coffee mug in his hands. His voice was as cold as his eyes when he asked if anyone had heard from his father.

The doctor shook his head.

"How long, Dr. Fischer?"

"I don't know, Jake."

"Bullshit! How long, Dr. Fischer?"

"A few hours at the most."

"Then I guess I had better get moving. Thanks for the coffee. And thanks for taking care of Mom. If I can ever repay you for all you've done, let me know how to do it."

"I will, son, I will."

Dr. Fischer dropped his head into his hands. All he could think about was what he'd seen in Jake St. Cloud's eyes.

7

Back in Selma St. Cloud's room, Jake looked at Nurse Gilligan and asked, "Is there anything you can do for my mother?" He looked around at the machines in the room.

"No, Jake, there really isn't. I wish there were."

"Okay, then, I'm taking over. I'll stay with her until . . . until I no longer have to stay. Thank you."

Nurse Gilligan stepped out of the room, tears spilling from her eyes. She didn't care. She looked up to see Dr. Fischer. "He said he'll take over." The doctor nodded as he led Nurse Gilligan to the doctors' lounge, where they sat down and had a good cry.

Jake's hold on his mother's hand was fierce. He prayed as he struggled with the prayers he'd learned as a child and more or less forgotten as he entered his teen years. Once he finally got the words out, it was easier to repeat them over and over and over. He didn't ask for life for his mother because he knew it was her time, but he did ask God to make the transition easy for her. He knew so little about life and death. He wished he knew more.

For five hours, Jake sat, prayed, and held his mother's hand. He didn't cry. He couldn't. When he heard the steady tone and saw the flat line on the monitor, he squeezed his mother's hand harder. He wasn't sure, but he thought he felt a return squeeze. Wishful thinking.

And then the room was full of people: Dr.

Fischer, Nurse Gilligan, and the crash team, which was waved away by the doctor.

What seemed like a long time later, but couldn't have been more than fifteen minutes, Aaron Fischer led Jake to his office.

"Tell me what to do now."

"Your father?"

"Forget about my father, Dr. Fischer. Tell me what to do, how to do it, and I will make all the preparations, and if my father should manage to show his face here anytime soon, tell him . . . tell him his wife's son has taken care of things. Can you deliver that message verbatim, Dr. Fischer?"

"I can, son. I will. Now, this is what you have to do . . ."

Chapter 1

Eighteen years later

Jake St. Cloud woke up with the queen mother of all hangovers. He cracked an eyelid and looked to his left. He saw that the space on the bed next to him was empty, but it was clear someone had slept there. He closed his eyes and tried to remember the night before. Then he decided, why bother. Playboy St. Cloud was back in the game. *I need to give this crap up,* he thought. *I'm getting too old to keep burning the candle at both ends.*

He needed to get up, to start the day. He groaned, the mere sound hurting his already throbbing head. He needed tomato juice and some aspirin, or some hair of the dog that bit

11

him the night before. *Shit, I wish I could remember.* He had been back in town only three days, and he was right back to square one. "That's it!" he bellowed at the top of his lungs, then wished he'd remained quiet.

Jake forced his legs over the side of the bed and, with every ounce of strength in his body, forced himself to his feet and headed for the shower. *What the hell am I doing back here, anyway?* Back here, in this case, meant Slidell, Louisiana. Oh yeah, his old man was in trouble, and he'd come home to gloat. Yeah, well, that made sense. Sort of. Kind of.

The truth was it was only part of the reason he had returned home. It was his thirty-fifth birthday, and his mother's lawyers had set up a meeting with him. A command performance, so to speak, at eleven o'clock that morning. That meant suit, tie, white shirt, polished shoes, and clear eyes. And he had to smell good.

Jake stepped into the shower and turned the water to ice cold. He almost passed out from the shock of twenty-seven different jets pounding bone-chilling water over his entire body. When he couldn't stand it a moment longer, he switched to hot, and again almost passed out from the shock. He finally adjusted the water to a normal temperature and soaped up. For one wild moment, he wished he could stay under the warm spray forever, or at least long enough to put his past behind him and start anew.

Maybe after the meeting that morning, he could do that. Since it was his birthday, didn't that mean a new beginning of sorts? In the scheme of things, he supposed it meant whatever a person wanted it to mean.

Out of the shower, Jake dried off, shaved, and got dressed. Down in the small kitchen of the house he'd bought when he finished college fourteen years ago, he made coffee. He looked around. He'd put in a new kitchen, fit for a bachelor, and a new bathroom on the second floor. Other than paint and new furniture, that was all he'd done. He'd wanted a home base to return to from time to time. Time to time translated into once a year, if that. Kindly, elderly neighbors looked after the property to supplement their retirement. The couple were the only people on the planet who had his private cell-phone number. Because old people took responsibility seriously, unlike the whippersnappers of today, the elderly couple felt dutybound to leave him messages at least once a week regarding his father and St. Cloud Oil, the oil company he owned. Jake was put off at first but gradually accepted that the Tiboudouxs meant well, and suffered through the long, wordy messages, then immediately forgot them.

Jake poured a large glass of tomato juice, then added some Tabasco and the juice of half a lime. He gulped at it as he washed down four aspirin. The Cajun coffee was thick, black, and strong. He hoped it would help his hangover and if not, oh well, tomorrow was another day. Like that was going to work. Today was what was important. It was the day he had to make some decisions, atone for . . . God, so many things. He'd not kept a single one of the promises he'd made to his mother. Not a one. Guilt rode his shoulders like a jockey riding a racehorse across the finish line. He had to make it all right, and he had to start immediately.

What was that old saying? Today is the first day of the rest of my life. Yeah, right.

He hadn't actually crashed and burned, but on occasion, he'd come too damn close for comfort. He'd done some productive things during the last eighteen years. He'd more than contributed. He'd finished college summa cum laude but only because he had book smarts. It all came easy, but he didn't have a lick of common sense, or at least that's what one of his professors had told him. The man had gone on to say that Jake had no life experiences to draw from. Jake had had too much respect for the professor to argue the point because he knew he was right.

So, he'd gone out to find those life experiences. He'd traveled the world, earned money working on oil rigs because he knew the oil business backward and forward. He'd gone from one end of the world to the other and, at least in terms of common sense, didn't have squat to show for it. *Life experience, my ass!*

Jake told himself not to be so hard on himself, because he'd done one good and serious
thing. He'd become a consultant to his father's
competitors and been very successful. He'd
also made the newspapers big-time. So much
so that his father, to no avail, had tried to muz-
zle him. Everyone wanted a piece of Jake St.
Cloud, even the Saudis. And the absolute best
part of his consulting business, which to his
mind was really a payback business, was that
he'd made so much money he couldn't count
it all. He had only one rule, and that was never
to work for St. Cloud Oil.

Now, though, Jake knew he had to get his
life back on track. And the thirty-fifth anniver-
sary of his birth was the first day down that
road. He poured a second cup of coffee and
drank it standing up by the counter. He realized then that he felt halfway decent.

When he finished the coffee, he put the cup
in the dishwasher. For a full minute he de-
bated whether he should turn on the dishwasher for just one cup. His mother's words
about cleanliness being next to godliness rang
in his ears. He shrugged, dropped a soap pel-
let in the machine, and turned it on. He totally
forgot his mother's words about never leaving
the house with an appliance running.

He left the house and climbed into his sleek
black Porsche and headed to his meeting with
his mother's lawyers. As he tooled along, Jake
made a mental note to get rid of the fancy

wheels and get himself a Dodge Ram pickup truck. And a dog to ride shotgun.

The law firm of Symon and Symon was run by two brothers who had to be as old as Methuselah. They creaked when they walked, but they were razor-sharp when it came to the ins and outs of the law and safeguarding their clients' businesses and assets. Somehow, some way—Jake couldn't remember—he thought they were distant cousins of his mother. Elroy Symon and his brother, Estes Symon. Pillars of the community.

Both greeted Jake in their three-piece suits. Pants, jacket, and vest, complete with watch fobs. They smiled and welcomed him like an old friend. Never mind that they hadn't seen him in over ten years. They offered coffee and beignets, which Jake knew came from the Café Du Monde in New Orleans. He knew this because he remembered his mother's telling him that the lawyers prided themselves on serving them fresh every day. He declined.

"Then I guess it's time to get down to business," Estes said. Or maybe it was Elroy. Jake could never keep them straight. He wondered if they were twins. Funny how he didn't know that.

"You turn thirty-five today, Jacob. A milestone. How do you feel about it?" one of them asked.

"I'm okay with it. Not much I can do about it, either way."

"So, you're all grown up. We've followed your . . . ah . . . career to a certain extent, young man."

Crap, here it comes, Jake thought. He waited.

"Have you gotten all your lollygagging out of the way, son?"

Lollygagging? "Is that another way of asking me if I have sowed all my wild oats?"

"I guess you could say that," Elroy said. Or maybe it was Estes. "The reason we ask is because your mother said we weren't to turn over your inheritance until we were sure you could handle it. So, the question confronting us right now, this very minute, is whether you are ready to man up." This last was said so smartly, Jake blinked and realized the two old lawyers were dead serious.

"Yes," he said just as smartly. He almost saluted but thought better of it.

"We thought so," Estes said. Or maybe it was Elroy. "The minute you walked through our door, I could tell that you had had your come-to-Jesus meeting. It's the way it should be on your thirty-fifth birthday."

"Yes, sir," Jake said respectfully. "Tell me what I have to do, and I'll do it."

"Nothing, son. Per your mother's instructions, we did everything for you. All the accounts have been set up. Everything balances out to the penny. The brokerage accounts are extremely robust. Extremely. We took the liberty of compiling a balance sheet for you, just to make it easier for you to understand. I do have a question for you, Jacob. Other than your college tuition, you never took a penny from the personal trust. Why is that?"

Why indeed? "I had done nothing to earn it. I frankly thought that I didn't deserve it. It didn't feel right. So I made my own way."

"What about your mother's ancestral home, the plantation outside of town?"

"I haven't been there in years. What do you mean? It's a working cotton plantation. Do I need to do something?"

"Only if you want to. There's over a thousand acres that are not being utilized. You might want to give some thought to that. Think in terms of a thousand acres you are paying taxes on with no revenue coming in from it."

Jake nodded. "Did my mother ever indicate what she'd like done with the plantation?"

Elroy nodded, or maybe it was Estes. "She said you'd know what to do with it when the time came. Do you?"

Oh, Mom, where did that blind faith you had in me come from? "Right this moment, I have to say I don't have a clue."

"Well, I'm sure something will come to you. Just remember all those taxes."

"I do have a question for you," Jake said. "Did my father ever repay my mother for all that money she doled out to him to start him up in the oil business?"

"He did, Jacob, but it took him quite a few years. We had to hound him, and we did. We charged him interest, too. He had some fancy lawyers try to come after us, but Judge Broussard settled them down in a hurry. Henry Broussard was your mama's sixth or seventh cousin twice removed, if I remember correctly. He's gone now, God rest his soul, at the age of ninety-four," Elroy said, or maybe it was Estes.

"If everything is in order, sign all those papers, and you can leave. We'll leave you alone for a few minutes so you can . . . adjust to all of this," one of the brothers said, motioning to the stacks of papers on the old table. The lawyers left the room.

Jake longed for a cigarette but remembered he'd quit smoking years ago. He looked down at the lone sheet of paper that summed up his net worth. He was glad he was sitting down, because he would have fallen over at seeing the bottom line. And he'd thought the oil business was profitable. The words *money to burn* ricocheted around and around inside his head. He was starting to get dizzy at what he was seeing and the responsibility that was suddenly on his shoulders.

Soon after Jake had finished signing the papers, the door opened, and the two brothers walked in and sat down again. "My brother, Estes, and I were talking outside. Years ago, we never could decide between the two of us if we should tell you this or not. At the time, we felt you were too young, and you were grieving for your mother, so we thought it best if we just left things alone."

"And now you think I'm old enough to know, is that it?" Jake asked.

"Well, today is your birthday. Thirty-five years of age *almost* guarantees some sort of wisdom on your part. During the last months of your mother's life, your father tried his best to get your mother to give him power of attorney. We simply could not allow that to happen. Your mother agreed. Your father threatened all manner of dire things, but he had no wish to go up against Henry Broussard again. Henry was still alive and sitting on the bench at that point. We just thought you should know."

"Did my father need money?"

"We checked, and the answer is no. Some people don't know when enough is enough. It's no secret, young man, that my brother and I do not hold your father in high regard. I'm sorry to tell you that."

Jake laughed. "Well, gentlemen, join the club. Thanks for all the hard work on my behalf and thank you for taking care of my mother's business so well."

"We were paid to do it. When you're paid for something, you do the best you can for monies received. We thank you for your business, son, and if there's anything you need us to do, we're here six days a week. You can call us on our mobile on Sundays but not till after church. Your mother was a fine lady, a wonderful mother, and a good friend."

"Yes, she was," Jake said with a lump in his throat. He stood, offered his hand, and was surprised at the firm, solid handshakes of the two brothers.

Outside, in the hot, humid air, Jake yanked at his tie, pulled it off, and stuffed it into the pocket of his jacket. At his car, he removed his jacket and threw it across to the passenger seat before driving back to his little house on the tree-shaded street.

When he got home, he headed to the second floor, stripped down, and pulled on cargo shorts and an old LSU T-shirt from his college days, which was so soft and worn that it felt like a second skin. His feet went into Birkenstocks and off he went. His next stop was Leona Sue's flower shop, and then on to St. Patrick's Cemetery.

Sweat was dripping down Jake's face when he entered Leona Sue's flower shop. He looked around at the profusion of flowers. His mother had always loved flowers, white roses being her favorite. She'd had a wonderful, beautiful flower garden when he was a boy. Mika, the gardener, had helped her with the compost and the peat moss and taught her all he knew, which was a lot. Mika always told her she had the prettiest roses in all of Louisiana. He made a mental note to check on Mika in his retirement.

A young girl, probably the owner's daughter, smiled and asked how she could help him.

"Do you have any white roses?"

"Believe it or not, we actually do. Not much call for them, but some came in yesterday. They're in the cooler. How many would you like? Oh, are they for delivery or are you taking them with you? We charge for delivery."

"I'll be taking them with me. How many do you have?"

"Let me look. Mom might have sold some of them after I left yesterday. I'll be right back."

Jake walked around, savoring the smell of the potted plants and the bright colors. He liked the smell. He turned when he heard the young girl shout from the back room where the cooler was. "I have three and a half dozen, sir!"

"Good! I'll take them all," Jake shouted in return.

"Would you like some greenery and baby's breath in the mix?"

Jake smiled. The young girl probably thought he didn't know what baby's breath or greenery meant, but he did. "Absolutely. Make it pretty."

When the young girl returned from the back room, her arms full of roses, Jake grinned. She'd wrapped them in green tissue, and they really were an armful. Jake thanked her and paid with his credit card.

The flowers took up the entire passenger seat. Now, if he had a dog, the dog would have had to sit on his lap. *Damn, where are these thoughts coming from?*

Jake drove with the window down because he hated air-conditioning in a car. For some reason, he always got a sinus infection when he turned it on. Recycled air, someone had once told him. The air outside was thick with humidity, but he didn't care.

Twenty minutes later, Jake drove down the road to the cemetery. He parked and walked to where his mother's final resting place waited for him. It was a quiet place. But then, all cemeteries were quiet places. He had helped Mika plant a young tree the day after his mother had been laid to rest. In eighteen years, the sapling had grown into a tall, sturdy young tree, with branches that resembled a giant umbrella. It created a canopy of shade over the bench Mika had helped him build out of mahogany, and he was stunned to see how the stout bench had survived the elements. The plot of grass was so green it shone like a giant emerald. Mika must still come out here to water and to clip the grass. To Jake's eye, it was the tidiest grave site in the whole cemetery. He marveled at how each blade of grass seemed to be the exact same length. Mika was a perfectionist. The stone was simple black marble, and he'd had the stonecutter carve an angel in the middle of it. The lettering was simple: his mother's name, the date of her birth, and the date of her death; and underneath, the inscription, MOTHER OF JACOB. He wondered, and not for the first time, if there had ever been any gossip or feedback when the name *St. Cloud* had been omitted. If there had been, no one told him, and he didn't really care one way or the other.

Jake sat down cross-legged and stared at the graceful angel, her wings spread protectively over a babe in a cradle. In his mind, he was the babe in the cradle. Tears burned his eyes. He made no move to wipe them away. They splattered down on the roses like the first morning dew.

He talked then of everything and nothing as he tried to play catch-up. It wasn't that he hadn't been there in the last eighteen years—he'd been many times, but all he'd done during those visits was leave some flowers and say a prayer that his mother's soul was resting in peace. This time, though, he owed her an accounting—an accounting he was not proud of. He didn't try to shield himself or make excuses. He owned up to everything.

"I feel like a real shit, Mom. I didn't keep one promise I made to you. Well, maybe one— I finished college, then took it on the lam. I think I went around the world at least three times. I was searching . . . for what I have no clue. The truth is, I was running away as hard and as fast as I could. It was so hard after you . . . after you were gone. I had a hell of a blowup with *him*. I said hateful, unforgivable things to the man who is my father. I told him he was a sperm donor. I really pissed him off, Mom, when I told him there had been a time when I had wanted to be like him. God, was that funny. You know what, Mom? He called me an ungrateful little bastard. He said I was a wuss, a mama's boy. I took it, Mom. I didn't argue or fight back. That day. But on another day, when they read your will before I left for college, we had it out, right there in the lawyers' offices. I reamed him a new one. I'm not being disrespectful here, Mom; I'm just trying to be as honest as I can because I'm here to ask your forgiveness. I know that a mother's love is unconditional, but I have to ask, just the same, because I can't forgive myself. Maybe I never will be able to grant that to myself. I told him I knew all about his women and how he was with one of them when you were dying. He didn't deny it.

"I tried, Mom, to find the woman named Sophia. I hired a dozen different detective agencies, and they all came up dry. I barged into his office one day and asked him point-blank who Sophia was. I saw, for just a nanosecond, a spark in his eye that confirmed there was someone named Sophia, but he called me delusional. I asked him how many illegitimate children he had. He called security and had my ass booted out of the office.

"Today is my birthday. I wish you were here to bake me a cake and help me blow out the candles. Thirty-five candles is a lot to blow out by oneself. I'd give my right arm if you could somehow magically appear to wish me a happy birthday! I'm turning over a new leaf and turning my life around, Mom. I mean it this time. I meant it the last time, too, but somehow I lost my way. I am so sorry, Mom. Estes and Elroy asked me if I was done lollygagging, and I said yes. I mean it, Mom. I'm going to do it all now, everything I didn't do the first time around. I just want to tell you how sorry I am that I let you down. It won't happen again. I need you to believe that. It would help if you'd find a way to give me a sign that you believe me and forgive me."

Jake sat for a long time, sweat dripping from his forehead and mingling with his tears. He was just about to get up when he saw a yellow butterfly perch on the angel's wing. A sign? He reached out a trembling hand, and the butterfly settled itself on his index finger. "Thanks, Mom!" He held his hand up, and the butterfly took wing. "That's good enough for me!" He blew a kiss in the direction of the angel, stood, and turned to leave. "I'll be back soon, Mom."

He saw *him* then, walking among the stones, weaving his way toward Jake.

"I thought I'd find you here," was all *he* said by way of a greeting.

"I'm sorry I can't say the same thing about you. This is the last place I ever expected to see *you*."

The two men, one old, one young, locked eyeballs. They were an even match, inch for inch, pound for pound. Jonah St. Cloud reached for his son's arm. Jake shook him free. "You don't want to do that again, and if you do, I'll forget who you are and deck your ass so that you can't walk for a month."

Jonah St. Cloud ignored his son's words. "I need to talk to you, Jake."

Jake walked away.

"Did you hear me, *boy*?"

Jake clenched his fists at his sides. He could feel his body start to shake, and he couldn't stop the tremors. He knew right that minute that he was capable of killing. He jammed his hands into his pockets. He turned around. "How did you know I would be here?"

"Simple. Today is your birthday. You turned thirty-five. You were born at seven twenty in the morning. You were bald as a cue ball and weighed seven pounds eight ounces, normal size back then. You were twenty-one inches long and had big feet. It was the proudest day of my life. You're in town to sign the papers so you can inherit your mother's estate. I figured it stood to reason you'd find your way here at some point today. I was prepared to wait all day if necessary."

"Why now? Why today? You want Mom's money, is that it? You figure you're going to throw a guilt trip on me and I'll just . . . what?

Hand it over? Man, you are one sick, sorry son of a bitch if that's what you're thinking."

"That's not what I'm thinking, and it's not what I want. I need your help, Jake."

"Well, that's not going to happen anytime soon. I wouldn't lift a finger to help you if you were dying. How's that grab you? Why would you ask me, of all people, to help you?" Jake asked, more out of curiosity than anything else.

"It doesn't grab me too well. And the reason I'm asking you is because you're my son."

"Oops! Guess you missed that part about your being my sperm donor. Sperm donors have no rights. Kiss my ass, *Dad.*"

Jonah St. Cloud flinched. "Name your price."

"Did I hear you right? Name my price? Well, you know what, I do have a price. If you're willing to pay it, then I'll be willing to listen to you, and maybe—I said maybe—help you out of whatever jam you've gotten yourself into."

"Name it, and it's yours. If you agree to help me."

Jake took all of two seconds to come up with his response. "Last name, address, phone number, and name of the child belonging to Sophia."

Jonah St. Cloud's face drained, but he didn't miss a beat when he said, "Sophia Rosario. The address is four twenty-two Aspen Lane in Slidell and the phone number is in the book.

The boy's name is Alexander Luther Rosario. He was born on the Fourth of July. He's four years younger than you, which makes him thirty-one."

Jake lost whatever control he had thought he had. His fist shot out, and his father toppled to the ground. Right then, he wanted nothing more than to pummel the man till he was a bleeding, hulking mess. Instead, he turned and went to his car. When he got in, the thick, heady scent of the roses he'd brought, mixed with the heavy humidity, lingered on the leather seat, making him gag.

"You gave me your word," Jonah shouted as he struggled to his feet.

"I lied!" Jake shot back as he gunned the horsepower under the hood. He would have taken off like a bat out of hell, but he saw the yellow butterfly settle itself in the middle of his windshield. He stared at it, then across to the space where the black marble angel hovered over the babe in the cradle. He sucked in his breath and whispered, hoping the butterfly heard him, "Okay."

A second later, the delicate little creature was airborne and out of his line of vision. He couldn't be sure, but he thought the beautiful little creature flew back to perch on the angel's wing.

Jake leaned out of the car window and said, "That was just so rude of me. Whatever *was* I thinking? I don't know what got in to me, *Dad.* What that means is, don't call me, I'll call you." And he would, because at the age of thirty-five, the new Jake St. Cloud was a man of his word.

Chapter 2

Jake turned off the highway and into a St. Cloud gas station. He pulled to the side and just sat there. *Did I just deck my father?* He looked down at his throbbing hand—all the proof he needed that he'd done just that. *What the hell was I thinking? What was it? Thirty-five years of pent-up rage?*

Was it because of the way his father had treated his mother, and this was payback for his betrayals? Or was it all the father-son things he'd wanted that had never happened during his growing-up years? Maybe it was that he'd been forced to work at the drilling sites during the summer and all vacation days? And to think that, somewhere in the back of his mind, at one time he'd wanted to grow up to be just like his father. *What a crock.*

Jake massaged his throbbing hand. He felt ashamed at what he'd done. But at the moment he'd let his clenched fist fly, the man he was aiming at wasn't his father. He was a man who had betrayed his wife. A man who couldn't be bothered to be at her side when she died. A father who was never there for his son. A sperm donor. He'd let his seventeen-year-old son make all the funeral arrangements. It still boggled Jake's mind that he'd even shown up at the service for his wife. The son of a bitch had even managed to squeeze out a tear. And then he was gone, leaving Jake standing alone, with only Estes and Elroy Symon to provide comfort.

Jake took great gulping breaths as he struggled to gain control of his emotions. Everything else aside, now he finally had the name of his half brother and his address. That alone was worth whatever consequences there were from the confrontation with his father.

The address was burned into his brain. He typed it into his GPS, headed for the gas pump, and filled the Porsche.

Twenty-three minutes later, the robotic voice on the GPS told him that he was eighteen feet from his destination. Jake drove around the block twice, trying to get a feel for the neighborhood. He decided it was a great place to raise kids. There were sidewalks; humongous trees shaded the front lawns and the sidewalks as well. Old-fashioned lampposts were on every corner. All the houses were well maintained, the lawns mowed, and the flower beds just perfect. If he hadn't known better, he would have thought Mika worked the neighborhood on his off-hours. The house itself was a ranch with diamond-paned windows. The front door was a cheery yellow that matched the yellow cushions on the two chairs on the small front porch. He could see pots of late-summer flowers lining the walkway to the front door. The house itself was painted white and had dark hunter-green shutters and trim. The white paint sparkled in the bright sunlight. He wasn't sure, but he thought the house looked freshly painted.

Here goes nothing, Jake thought as he climbed out of the car that he had parked on the street in front of the house. He walked to the door and was not the least bit surprised to see that there were no weeds in the lawn. He wondered if anyone would be home at that hour of the day. Surely, the mother and son worked.

That's when he noticed the Mustang convertible sitting in the driveway. He'd been so taken with the house, he hadn't seen it at first. *Okay, Mom, I'm here. I'm going to try to make it right.*

Jake rang the doorbell. Five musical notes could be heard. A welcome to visitors.

The door opened, and Jake stared at a mirror image of his father. His jaw dropped. The young man standing in the open doorway, his tie askew, his shirtsleeves rolled up, stared at Jake as though he knew him.

"I'm . . ."

"I know who you are. Jake St. Cloud."

Damn, the guy even sounds like the old man. "Yeah, that's me. Look, I'm not sure what the protocol is here. I just found out about you forty-five minutes ago. I came straight here."

"Why?"

"Because years and years ago, on her death-bed, my mother asked me to find you. I tried. She herself had tried for years, too, before she passed. All we had was what we thought was your mother's name—Sophia. My mother wanted me to know she thought I had a brother or a sister. She didn't want me to be alone after she was gone."

Alex Rosario slouched against the door frame as he eyed his half brother. "You weren't exactly alone now, were you? You had a father, which is more than I had, but I do have the best mother in the whole world."

"Back then, I would have fought you till one of us went down for saying that. I had the best mother in the whole world, too. I'm willing to concede the point, though. That father you might have anguished over not having? Give it up. He wasn't a father, he was just a sperm donor. Now, are you going to invite me in or not? It's got to be a hundred and ten degrees out here."

"Well, it's a hundred degrees in this house. Our A/C went out. That's why I'm here. I'm waiting for the technician. Come on in."

"You don't look like the sperm donor," Alex observed, leading the way into the cheeriest, homiest kitchen Jake had ever seen. "Do you look like your mother? Iced tea?"

"Whoa. Switch that up. You do look like him. I do take after my mother's side of the family. Which I think puts me one up on you. I was blessed, and you got cursed. I was born first, if that makes a difference. Yes on the iced tea."

The brothers sat down across from each other and eyed one another.

"Why are you here? What do you want? How did you find us?"

"I told you, I made a deal with the devil. Well, maybe I didn't exactly say that, but that's what I did. Meaning the devil is our mutual sperm donor. Until today, I hadn't spoken to Jonah St. Cloud since the day of my mother's funeral. He found me. Today is my birthday. I turned thirty-five, and I had some stuff I had to do with my mom's lawyers, and after that, I went to the cemetery to . . . to . . . to own up to my mom that I had failed to keep every damn promise I made to her on her deathbed, mainly the one about finding you and your mother.

"Just as I was leaving, the sperm donor showed up. Guess he kept track of things. He asked for my help. He told me to name my price. You were my price, and he gave it up. And here I am. Well, before I left, I knocked him on his ass. Then I came here."

Alex leaned across the table, his expression intense. "How did it feel?"

Jake grinned. "Liberating. I put everything I had into that punch. I wanted to keep beating him till he was a bloody pulp, but I didn't. I pulled into a gas station to calm down and felt ashamed for all of ten seconds."

"He just took it? He let you punch him out and didn't fight back? What kind of man is that?" Alex asked, his eyes wide in shock at what he was hearing.

"Think sperm donor, bro. Oh, he did ask when we would get together for the help he wanted from me. I told him I lied. All I wanted was your name. Just so you don't think I'm a complete shit, I will get in touch with him. My mother taught me better than that."

The doorbell rang. Alex excused himself and went to answer it. He was back in minutes. "A/C guy. Thank God! More tea?"

"Yeah, it's good."

"My mom makes it from different tea leaves. She owns the restaurant she used to work at when she met . . . And before you ask, she bought it working around the clock, and *he* didn't give a penny toward it. Actually, we just paid off the mortgage last year. That's how my mother met our . . . the sperm donor. She was a waitress and he swept her off her feet. She was only seventeen at the time. She doesn't . . . she just told me what she thought I needed to know back then when I had questions. I found out the rest over the years. I'm not getting any of this. What is it you want from us?"

"Not a damn thing. I want to do something for you and your mother. I told you, it's what my mother wanted. I promised her. So, tell me, what can I do for you?"

"Not a damn thing, *bro*. We're doing just fine on our own. This place," Alex said, waving his arm about, "might not be up to your standards, but it's how most of America lives. I wouldn't trade it for all the palatial mansions in the world."

Jake didn't like the sarcasm he was hearing in his brother's voice. He winced.

This wasn't going to be easy. He looked up when he saw a man in a baseball cap standing at the kitchen door. The tag on his shirt said A-1 REFRIGERATION.

"Mr. Rosario, I hate to be the bearer of bad news, but your unit is shot. You need a new one. I can have it installed tomorrow if you want."

"Crap!" Alex slapped at his forehead. "How much?"

"It will be seventy-two hundred dollars, including labor."

"Can't you jury-rig it?"

"It's been jury-rigged so many times, there's nothing left to jury-rig. So, what's it going to be? I got six more service calls today."

"Give me a few minutes; I need to call my mother to see what she wants to do."

Though he knew he should try not to listen, Jake strained to hear every word his brother was saying. The bottom line to Jake was that they didn't have that much cash on hand. He waited.

Alex ended the call. If he was embarrassed that Jake had heard any part of the conversation, he didn't show it. "What kind of installment plan do you have?"

"Twenty percent down and the rest spread over two years."

"Okay, order it. When do you want to do the paperwork?"

"Tomorrow, when I get here."

"That'll work."

When the door closed behind the technician, Alex said, "Where were we?"

"You were telling me you didn't need anything and middle America lives the way you and your mom live. I was about to agree with you and tell you how much I like this house, especially the kitchen. Growing up, my mother and I ate at this very long dining-room table. It sucked. I don't think she knew how to cook. My mother, that is. But she did make me hot cocoa when I was sick, and sometimes she made cookies. They were very good. She called them sugar cookies. They were like cake."

"Well then, let me tell you how it was here. Jonah St. Cloud had his lawyer give my mother just enough money for us to get by. He did pay Mom's hospital bills. My mother had to keep working and pay for day care when I was little.

As I got older and needed more stuff, a friend of hers convinced her to get a lawyer to ask for more money. The skunk tried to fight it, but Mom held firm, so he increased her monthly allotment. Not by much, but it did help. He only paid for a quarter of my college. Mom banked it because I worked my way through. That's how she was finally able to pay off the restaurant. I have to tell you, to this day, my mother never said a bad word about that man. I, on the other hand, let it rip, and she'd look at me with those big eyes of hers and tell me she was ashamed of me. So, you see, I know what that feels like. It was all her workers, who are incredibly loyal to my mother, who chipped in and bought me a clunker of a car when I was old enough to drive. I had to learn to be a mechanic because it kept breaking down. Mom says it all helped build my character."

Alex stood and started to unroll his sleeves. "Well, if we're done strolling down memory lane, I have to get back to the office. It was nice of you to stop by, bro."

"It *was* nice of me, now that you mention it. I have to wonder, if you were in my place, would you have done the same thing?"

"Probably not."

"Well, that's honest enough. I truly admire honesty in a person. What is it you do, Alex?"

"I'm a lawyer. I work with three other guys in a storefront office for people who need lawyers but can't afford them. As I said before, the sperm donor did not pay for my education. I worked my way through and had some grants. I'm still paying off student loans. I had a full-ride scholarship if I wanted to play football, but I turned it down."

"Why?"

Alex laughed. "Because my mother said she didn't want an idiot with a bad back and bad knees for a son. She said no. I know all about how you gave up five different scholarships back in the day. Maybe that made it easier for me to say no. Jesus, you have no idea how much I wanted to be you. You should have heard me cheering you at all those football games and not being allowed to tell anyone you were my brother. Pretty jerky, huh?"

"That hurts me, heart and soul. I swear to God it does. You knew about me, but I didn't know a damn thing about you or your mother. Until an hour or so ago."

"Yeah, well, don't let it get your panties in a knot. It all worked out just fine. As you can see." Alex held out his hand. Jake reached for it and wanted to cry so damn bad, he had to bite down on his lower lip. He wasn't sure, but he thought Alex was feeling something, too.

"Can I say one more thing?" Jake said.

"Sure, spit it out."

"I understand pride. I understand you don't want anything from me. That's fine. I'm okay with that, but your mother, from what you said, got the shitty end of the stick. It wasn't my fault, and it wasn't my mother's fault. It was my mother, another woman, who maybe understood what happened better than you or I ever could. She was dying, Alex, when she made me promise to find you and your mother. You want to be cavalier about all this, fine, but don't make that decision for your mother. That's not right."

They were outside by then, standing on the flower-bordered walkway, when Alex responded, "You know what I have trouble with? You're thirty-one years too late."

"Through no fault of my own. Be sure to say that."

"Right, through no fault of yours or your mother's."

"So, I just leave here, you go back to your storefront law office, and we call it a day?"

"That's pretty much how I see it," Alex said, opening his car door. "I promise to tell my mother you stopped by."

Jake nodded because he didn't trust himself to say any more. His eyes burned as he climbed behind the wheel of the Porsche. Jake waited until Alex backed out, waved, and was around the corner before he could turn the key. The engine growled to life, but he didn't move. *Well, Mom, that didn't go over very well. I tried. I don't know what to do now. I'm thinking I can't force myself on them. They're nice people, Mom, and they made it on their own. God, I have a kid brother. Who knew? It was strange how much he looks like Dad, and I look so much like you. Night and day.*

Jake waited for what he hoped would be a lightning bolt of wisdom, but none came. He was almost blinded by his own tears when he tore away from the curb and headed down the same street Alex had taken. He didn't see the white van backing out of the driveway because, at the exact moment of impact, a yellow butterfly settled itself in the middle of his windshield.

And that's when all hell broke loose. He felt the crash, felt his car do a one-eighty, heard the screams, saw people running out of their houses. He struggled out of the low-slung seat and ran to the white van. He almost fainted when he saw a slim blonde trying to undo her seat belt. He reached in and undid it for her. Then he looked in the back to see three frightened children, one in a car seat. He yanked at the door as the mother kept screaming, calling him every name in the book that ended with *maniac*.

Jake heard the sirens and the people who were screaming that he was doing eighty in a twenty-five-mile-per-hour residential zone. *Forty or fifty maybe, but not eighty.* He saw the ambulance, saw the EMTs rushing to the kids and the mother. He stood perfectly still as he waited for the cops, who were right on the ambulance's tail, to get out of the car. *God, please let them be okay. Please.*

Jake had his wallet out and withdrew his license and registration and insurance card.

"This your car, sir?" the cop asked, pointing to the Porsche.

"Yes, sir, it's mine." Jake handed over his credentials. The cop looked down at the name, then at the picture, and walked over to his partner to show him what he was holding. The second cop looked over at Jake. Ah, the St. Cloud name. He watched the heated argument between the two officers. He could still hear the neighbors demanding that they arrest him for reckless endangerment. *Guilty as charged.*

Jake almost blacked out when he heard the mother say she thought everyone was fine. One of the EMTs said he wasn't taking her word for it and loaded the excited kids into the back of the ambulance along with their mother. Sirens blaring, red and blue lights flashing, the ambulance left the street.

The first cop approached Jake. "We need to take you down to the station, Mr. St. Cloud. We'll take your statement there. I'm not going to handcuff you, so behave yourself. Okay?"

Jake nodded as he climbed into the backseat of the patrol car.

Jake knew he was getting preferential treatment. He wisely kept quiet as the second cop read him his rights. Then he was asked if he understood those rights, and he said he did. The ride to the police station was made in total silence.

Jake had never been inside a police station. He looked around. It smelled of sweat and burned coffee. From what he could gather, they were going to charge him with speeding and reckless endangerment. *Guilty on both counts. Lock me up and throw away the key. I deserve it.*

Jake signed the statement he'd given, which

was short and to the point. *I was driving faster than I should have been driving and didn't see the van until it was too late. I slammed on my brakes and spun around. That's it.*

"Why aren't you squawking for a lawyer?" a detective named Roscoe Logan asked.

"Why, do I need one? I'm guilty. What more do you want?"

"You could have killed those little kids," the detective said.

"I know that. I'm sorry. I know those are just words. If I had to do it over again, I'd drive five miles an hour. Look, I said I was guilty, so do whatever you have to do. Just tell me, are the mother and kids okay?"

"Yeah, for the most part. Shook up. They're getting checked out."

Jake nodded.

"Why do I have this feeling you're not telling me the whole story, sir?" the first cop asked.

Like there's some excuse I can trade on? Like, hey, I just found out a few hours ago I have a kid brother and I went to see him to do whatever I could for him and his mother because I broke a promise to my dying mom and I was trying to make it right and then this yellow butterfly alights on my windshield, the same butterfly that was at the cemetery—is that the kind of stuff I'm leaving out?

"That's my story, Detective. I'm guilty. Look, don't let my name influence you here. Don't go there, okay? I don't want to hear that the St. Clouds employ half this town. That's not me. I don't have anything to do with that. I take full responsibility for what happened."

"Okay, Mr. St. Cloud. We'll be booking you now. You'll have a bond hearing in the morning. You sure you don't want a lawyer? If you can't afford one, the court will appoint one for you."

"Nope. I'm good."

"You sure now, Mr. St. Cloud?"

"Just for the record, Detective, I'm not my old man, okay? I told you, I'm guilty, and I take full responsibility. Don't worry, the wrath of God will not descend on the police department by way of the St. Cloud name. I guarantee it."

The detective stared at Jake, his eyes showing his skepticism. "Then if you'll follow me, we can get you settled nice and tidy into a cell."

Bet you're so proud of me, Mom. I let you down again. Betcha five bucks my kid brother wouldn't have done what I just did.

Chapter 3

Eighty-year-old Nathan Broussard leaned back in his leather chair, his eyes on the black robe hanging on a coat tree near the door. In a few minutes, he had to go out into the courtroom for the last time. He wondered what he would encounter by way of a farewell in the place where he'd served over forty years, just as his brother, Henry, had served the people of Louisiana. Henry was a mean son of a bitch who went by the book and the letter of the law. Nathan, on the other hand, was a meaner son of a bitch who only went by the book when it served his purposes. No sense not calling a spade a spade when it was called for.

After court that day, he would attend his retirement party, then head off into the sunset with his wife of fifty-five years. That was what the press release said; a trip around the world that he'd promised his wife on the day they got married and every year since. What he was actually going to do was head to Rhode Island, where his seventy-seven-year-old brother, Franklin, ran an assisted living facility. All the paperwork had been completed months ago. Franklin had assured Nathan that he had the best doctors in the state on call to treat his Alzheimer's. On his last checkup, in Rhode Island, the specialists had told him he was in the first stage of the disease, but that his condition was aggressive, and further warned that he should not make any more rulings in his courtroom. That had scared the bejesus out of him. If word of his condition got out, every case he'd ruled on for the last ten years would become suspect. His wife, Agnes, his voice of reason, had minced no words and put their plan into action.

Time to go. Don't look back. You had a hell of a run, old boy. Get through today's court docket, attend your retirement party, and walk away. How simple that sounded. It was going to be the hardest thing he'd ever done in his life.

Nathan looked at the clock hanging directly in his line of vision. He still had ten minutes to finish his coffee and the article he had been reading in the *Times-Picayune* before his clerk helped him on with his robe and handed him the daily roster of who was to appear in front of him. His gaze dropped to the article he'd been reading about Angelica Dancer and her daughter, Fancy. He found it interesting that Angelica Dancer, a prima ballerina, had been struck down with rheumatoid arthritis at the height of her career. She'd studied with the Bolshoi and gone all the way. Nathan felt sorry for the woman just the way he felt sorry for himself, but after her diagnosis, she made a life for herself and her young daughter, Fancy, who later followed in her mother's dancing footsteps. The story should have had a happy ending at that point, but as Nathan read on, he saw that on the night of young Fancy's much-ballyhooed debut, the stage had collapsed, severely injuring her and several other dancers. Young Fancy's career ended as tragically as her mother's. Neither woman would ever dance again.

While Angelica Dancer was confined to a wheelchair, and young Fancy was crippled and scarred, neither woman had given up. They ran and operated the Dancer Foundation, a home for abused and battered children. They'd started small and currently operated a facility, right there in St. Tammany Parish, that was filled to capacity with twenty-five children. According to Angelica, they needed more volunteers and more contributions. Fancy had added that they were desperate for volunteers because they found it impossible to turn any child away.

"Joseph," Nathan called to his clerk, "did you read this article on the Dancer ladies?"

"I did, Your Honor, before I left the house

to come to work. My wife said she's going to pledge two days a week to the ladies and that maybe some of her bingo partners might join her. It's sad that two such beautiful women should have such tragedy in their lives. I guess it's true what they say. When the Lord gives you lemons, make lemonade. Here's the roster. A full day, Your Honor."

Nathan shrugged into his black robe and snapped it shut. His watery gaze raked the list of names on the roster. He stopped at the third name and squinted. Jacob St. Cloud. His back stiffened, and his eyes turned cold and hard.

St. Tammany Parish Judge Nathan Broussard swooped into his courtroom to hear the most beloved words in his vocabulary: "All rise! The Honorable Judge Nathan Broussard presiding."

Judge Broussard made short work of the first two cases that came before him. It was a record even for him. His law clerk frowned, as did the bailiff.

The bailiff called the third case on the docket. "The State of Louisiana versus Jacob St. Cloud."

"Beth Goins for the prosecution," a pretty blond woman said, addressing the judge.

"Who is counsel for the defense?" the judge asked, peering over the top of his glasses at the people in the courtroom.

Jake got to his feet and was about to speak when he heard three different voices.

"Alex Rosario for the defense." His voice was drowned out by two other voices.

"Estes Symon for the defense."

And then, "Elroy Symon for the defense."

"Well, which is it?" Judge Broussard growled, his unhappiness apparent to all in the courtroom.

"I'm defending myself, Your Honor," Jake said. "I didn't hire anyone. I'm pleading guilty."

"No, he's not pleading guilty," Rosario said.

"He certainly is not," Estes and Elroy Symon said at the same time.

Judge Broussard leaned forward as though he were going to pop over the top of his desk. "I will not have a mockery made of this court. Now, one at a time, who is counsel for the defense?"

Jake looked around, his face a dark cloud. "They mean well, Your Honor, but I did not hire them. I am my own counsel. I plead guilty."

"Did you ever hear the saying that when a man represents himself, he has a fool for a client?" Judge Broussard snapped.

"No, Your Honor, I never heard that. I guess I'm a fool then."

"Asshole," Alex Rosario hissed between his teeth. "This is the meanest, the orneriest judge in the state. Don't go pissing him off now," he continued.

Estes, or maybe it was Elroy, stepped forward and leaned on his seventy years of friendship with Nathan Broussard. "The boy is in shock, Nathan. He doesn't know what he's doing. We have represented him for all his life. We can't walk away from him now."

Damnation, this isn't supposed to be happening. "I'm calling a ten-minute recess for all of you to decide what you're doing. A warning to all of you: do not try my patience." The judge banged his gavel extra hard to make his point before he swooped off his seat like some dark-cloaked avenger.

Back in his chambers, Judge Broussard looked at his longtime, loyal clerk. "Well, if that isn't a fine howdy do!"

"What are you going to do, Your Honor?"

"For starters, if those three lawyers open their mouths again, I'm going to find them in contempt. The kid said he was his own attorney, and that's good enough for me. Now, this is what I want you to do. Listen . . ."

Back in the courtroom, Judge Broussard settled himself at his bench. He was pleased to see that the three attorneys had taken seats in the back of the courtroom. Jacob St. Cloud remained seated at the defense table alone.

"Will the defendant please rise!"

Jake stood up, ramrod stiff. Out of the corner of his eye, he saw the door open and his father step through. *Shit.*

"Do you still want to plead guilty, Mr. St. Cloud?"

"I do, Your Honor."

"Are you asking for bail?"

"No, sir, I'm not."

"Then are you ready to be sentenced?"

Jake tried to stand even taller. "Yes, Your Honor."

"You admit you were driving at an excessive rate of speed."

"Yes, Your Honor."

"You realize that you were lucky this time that no one was seriously injured. There were children and a young mother in that vehicle."

"Yes, Your Honor, I realize that."

"Do you have anything to say in your own defense, Mr. St. Cloud?"

"No, Your Honor."

"There are a number of ways I can sentence you, young man. But first I want to ask you a question. How does a year in jail sound?"

Jake almost blacked out. "Not good, Your Honor, but if that's your sentence, I'll accept it."

"How about a ten-thousand-dollar fine?"

"I'll pay it, Your Honor."

"How does a year's probation working and living at a shelter for abused children sound to you? Along with a fifty-thousand-dollar donation to the shelter? At the end of the year, your record would be expunged. You would be assigned a parole officer with whom you will have to check in once a week."

"That's fine, Your Honor."

The judge leaned forward again and stared out over the courtroom. "Mr. Rosario, in your zeal to represent this man I am now giving you another chance. I'm appointing you his personal parole officer. You will send a report to my replacement, whoever that might be, once a week. I'm not taking no for an answer, Mr.

Rosario. Mr. St. Cloud, I am waiting for your response."

Jake blinked. It was a question. "I thought I did answer it. I said it was fine with me. I can handle that, Your Honor." *In a pig's eye, I can handle that.*

"Consider it done then, Mr. St. Cloud. Tomorrow morning, at precisely seven o'clock, you will report to the Dancer Foundation. The deputies will come by your house and transport you there. And you will remain there for one full year from today, occupying whatever accommodations are provided for you. You are not allowed to use any of your own funds to make life more comfortable. Is all that understood? I'm cutting you some slack here, Mr. St. Cloud, so you can return to your home, get cleaned up, and gather your things."

Jake nodded before he was led away by two deputies.

"Next case!" Judge Broussard bellowed as his gaze locked with that of Jonah St. Cloud.

In the anteroom outside the courtroom, the three lawyers rushed at Jake. "What the hell were you thinking in there?" Alex demanded. "I could have gotten you off, you dumb schmuck."

"Well, that doesn't sound like justice to me. I did it, okay? I'm guilty. What part of that don't you get? I deserve to be punished. At least I didn't get jail time. How the hell did you know I was here, anyway?"

"Are you kidding? Every person on our

street called my mother at the restaurant to tell her. She called me. I tried to get in to see you last night, but it didn't happen."

"Who is this person?" Elroy asked, or maybe it was Estes. "We've been your attorney of record since the day you were born. We could have reasoned with the judge. He's a friend and a distant relative."

"For starters, this guy standing here is my brother. You got that? *My brother!* Yeah, I know you didn't know that, but it's true. Take a good look at him. He looks just like my father. I don't want any favors called in. I did a dumb-ass stupid thing, and now I am going to pay for it. And well I should."

For the first time in their lives, the Symon brothers went silent.

"What the hell happened yesterday? If I had even an inkling you were suicidal, I never would have left you. You looked okay to me when I left. What the hell would make you speed on a street like mine? Did something happen, or did I just get under your skin?"

Jake shrugged. "I wasn't suicidal. There was this . . . this butterfly . . ."

"What the hell?" Alex said.

"Okay, okay, this is what happened . . ." Jake recounted the events that led up to the accident.

"Yes, then it was a good thing you did plead guilty," Estes said, or maybe it was Elroy. "No one, least of all Nathan, would have believed a story like that. But we do believe it, don't we, Elroy?"

"Yes, yes, we believe you, son. So how do we make out the check to the place where you will be spending your next year?"

"You don't. I'll pay it myself out of my own money. Thanks for showing up. You, too, bro. Sorry you got nominated as my parole officer."

"Ah, hell, I have a lot of free time."

"Did you show up so I'd have to pay you a retainer, so you could use that money for the twenty percent down payment on your new A/C unit?" In spite of himself, Jake burst out laughing at the expression on Alex's face.

"Nah, well, yeah, sort of, but my mother made me come. You happy now?"

Jake laughed again.

A deputy entered the room and said, "Sit down, Mr. St. Cloud, so I can fit you with this ankle monitor."

"Say what?" Jake exploded.

"Oh yeah, ankle monitors are Judge Broussard's favorite thing in life. He never tells the defendant he's getting one. He loves surprises. I told you he was an evil, nasty, cantankerous old buzzard. Just for the record, you'll never get used to it. It's going to itch and chafe, but you're stuck with it. The other surprise he didn't tell you is that he lifted your driver's license for a year. He's a real cutup, that judge." At Jake's look of outrage Alex laughed. "You know what they say—you play, you pay. One way or another."

The Symon brothers looked like two precocious squirrels as they watched Jake being fitted with the ankle monitor. Both grumbled that it was ugly and cumbersome.

"In case you didn't see him, the sperm donor showed up as you were being sentenced. He gave me the evil eye, and I gave it right back. Just so you know. I wouldn't want to be keeping any secrets from you at this point," Alex said.

"You're an asshole, Alex. I saw him."

"That's my line. One last thing, Jake. You can't leave the premises once you're taken to the Dancer Foundation. And you cannot have guests visiting you. I'll get a transcript of everything and bring it out to you when I check on you next week. You are going to have to retain me, however. I might be able to appeal a few things, like your leaving the premises if someone drives you, or the part about people visiting you. And we might be able to get the judge to allow you to use your own money to improve your accommodations. No promises, though. Depends who they name as Broussard's replacement."

"Yeah, okay. Thanks."

"Don't thank me; thank my mother. She threatened to snatch me bald if I didn't show up to represent you."

"Well, then, thank her for me. You seem to do better at following orders than I ever did."

"See you, Jake." Alex clapped him on the back and left by a side door.

"I guess we should leave, too," Elroy said, or maybe it was Estes. "We will keep watch on you, son. Do a good job, and the time will go quickly. And then you can get your life back. Was that story really true about the butterfly?"

Jake was suddenly very tired. He'd spent the entire night in the lockup guarding his person from the derelicts he was rooming with, and now he could barely keep his eyes open. He nodded.

Jake was taken out a side door, ushered into a patrol car, and driven home, with the deputies reminding him they would be on his doorstep at six thirty in the morning. Jake didn't bother to respond. He entered his house, locked the doors, and headed for the shower, where he scrubbed down no less than four times to make sure no bugs or lice were crawling over him. Then he climbed into bed and slept till almost midnight. He woke refreshed, took another long, hot shower, and went downstairs to make himself something to eat, after which he packed his things in a huge duffel and set it by the front door for his early-morning departure.

Jake spent the remaining hours in his darkened living room swilling cup after cup of coffee as he contemplated his past, the present, and what the future held for him.

Just five miles away, Angelica and Fancy Dancer started their new day as they prepared for their new twenty-four/seven, 365-day volunteer, compliments of just-retired St. Tammany Parish Judge Nathan Broussard.

Fancy Dancer was a beautiful young woman with ebony hair and liquid brown eyes. There was a tint to her skin that made the wicked scar, running from her eyebrow down the side of her cheek, stand out. Sometimes, when she had time to waste, she would apply thick theatrical makeup to cover the scar. She had a glorious smile that was capable of lighting up a room. When she was tired, which was most of the time, a decided limp could be seen in her gait. After one meeting with the graceful, beautiful young dancer, one ceased to see the scar or notice the limp. She was just Fancy. In the beginning, after the accident and all the operations, she'd tried to hide the scar by letting her hair cover it, and she'd practiced standing a certain way so people wouldn't notice when she limped, and pity her.

That all ended when she'd become so depressed that her mother took charge, pep-talked her, and proved to her daughter that just because you're handicapped does not mean that you can't have a good life. So, with the money Angelica had saved from her years of performing in every major ballet venue in the world, she'd encouraged Fancy to use her accident settlement monies, which amounted to a robust sum, to buy this very piece of property and take in what they called the throwaway kids. They'd started small, with just six children, and over the past seven years that number had increased to twenty-five youngsters they loved, nurtured, and looked after.

Their only problem, aside from needing more money each year, was finding people willing to donate their time. The kids themselves helped, the older children taking the younger ones under their wing. Schedules were set up and followed. They had their own school in one of the old barns on the property. Retired seniors who had been teachers in their other lives rotated their schedules to home school the kids. While it wasn't an elite academy, not even close, the kids were learning and doing their best in a loving environment, and what more could anyone want?

Stores and restaurants, when they found out about the foundation or saw an ad asking for donations, gave food by the bushel and carton. There were times when they had too much and times when they didn't have enough, but somehow they managed.

There was nothing modern at all about the Dancer Foundation. More often than not the plumbing stopped working or the electricity went out. Just about everything at the foundation carried three or four layers of duct tape, which they were never without.

They had one television set because Fancy said they needed computers more than they needed to watch television. Reading was stressed, and trips to the local library were encouraged. All in all, when the authorities came by for their usual inspections, the reports were glowing and satisfying. Those same reports were always followed up with the inspector saying he or she didn't know how the two Dancer women did it, considering their disabilities, but they were doing it. And if they overlooked the duct tape, so what?

"Mom, where are we going to put this guy when he gets here? We're so stretched for room now, there's just no place for him. He's a guy, so he's going to need some kind of space and privacy."

Angelica, Angel to her friends, looked up at her daughter. "I've been thinking about nothing else since Judge Broussard called yesterday. The only thing I can think of is that we'll get him a cot, and he'll have to sleep in one of the schoolrooms. He can come over here to shower and shave, that kind of thing. We'll tell him he has to get up an extra hour earlier than everyone else. We can't be unkind to him, even though this is a punishment. And it will be nice to have a man here to help out. I've seen pictures of him, you know. He's a handsome young man, he really is. He comes from serious money. Oil money," she said in a hushed voice.

"He's a playboy, Mom. He has a different woman on his arm every night, and he drives a fancy sports car that cost more than it takes to run this place for a whole year. I saw those same articles and pictures. Don't go getting your hopes up that this guy is going to save our butts. We'll probably be cracking his to get him to do some honest work. Everyone isn't fit to take care of kids. Even we have our bad days, and we both love kids. To be honest, Mom, I'm not looking forward to our new volunteer. And he's coming with an ankle monitor. He can't drive for a year; they took his license. So he isn't going to be a help to us when it comes to driving."

"I don't share your feelings, Fancy. I think it's all going to work out just fine. Do you think you can give me my shot now?"

Fancy smiled. "Sure, Mom. She reached inside the refrigerator and pulled out the needle with Humira. She plunged it into the softness of her mother's stomach, rinsed the needle, then wrapped it in a plastic grocery bag before she threw it in the trash. "It's wearing off quicker these days, isn't it?" she asked, concern ringing in her voice. She felt her mother's pain each time she looked at her swollen hands and feet.

Angel sighed. She never could fool that astute daughter of hers. "Sometimes. I'll make the coffee, you start the cereal. Five more minutes and he should be here."

"Oh, gee whiz, Miz Angelica, I can hardly wait for that white knight to come knocking on our door to save us two beautiful damsels. Yessiree, I can hardly wait."

Angel laughed and pointed to the back

door. "I think the white knight just arrived on his trusty, or should I say the parish's, four-wheel steed."

"Oh, this is going to be good," Fancy said, her grin spreading from ear to ear. "Wait till Bobby lets all the dogs loose!"

"Oh dear, I did forget about our other housemates. Well, that's just something else our new volunteer will have to get used to, now won't he?"

"Yep, guess so."

Angel didn't miss the giggle in her daughter's throat. She couldn't remember the last time she'd heard Fancy giggle. Or laugh, or even smile. Maybe the new volunteer could help that situation. Maybe.

Chapter 4

Jake looked over his new residence with a jaundiced eye. It was a big, sprawling house with additions going every which way. It almost looked like a puzzle with pieces missing.

"I have to officially hand you over to the ladies," the deputy said, his tone just short of embarrassed.

"No problem," Jake said as he craned his neck to look around. It was a nice setting, with old oak trees dripping Spanish moss. Peaceful. Restful. Here and there, he could see some grass. Just patches. The place needed Mika's fine hand. The shrubs had been pruned at some point. Compared to a nine-by-six cell, this was definitely a better deal.

Jake hefted his two duffel bags out of the

trunk and slung them over his shoulder. He wished he'd taken the time to eat something. His stomach was growling. He followed the deputy, who was ringing the doorbell. The front door was opened by a woman sitting in a wheelchair. Her voice was soft and melodious when she said, "Please, come in."

The deputy waited until she turned her chair around, then said to Jake, "Follow me."

Jake followed the deputy inside and looked around. The house was old, the furnishings just as old, but everything looked clean and comfortable. From somewhere overhead, he heard children's voices. *Happy* children's voices.

In the old-fashioned kitchen, introductions were made. Jake set his duffels down and was about to shake hands with the woman in the wheelchair when he saw her swollen, disfigured hands. She smiled and said, "I'm sorry."

The words just flew out of Jake's mouth. "It looks painful. Is it?"

"Very," Angelica said quietly.

"I'm Fancy, and yes, that's my real legal name," Fancy said, a touch of defiance ringing in her voice. Suddenly, she wished she'd taken a few more minutes with her hair and maybe used some of the concealer makeup she used for special occasions. *Vanity, thy name is woman.* She couldn't remember the last time she'd seen anyone so good-looking staring at her. Or at her scar. Normally, the stares didn't bother her, but she had to fight the urge not to bring her hand up to cover the ugly blemish on her face.

The deputy handed Fancy a clipboard. "Just sign at the bottom, Ms. Dancer. It just says I am releasing Mr. St. Cloud into your custody." He almost said *he's your problem now,* but he didn't. Instead, he nodded to the two women, then turned and walked away.

The silence was awkward. And then it was pandemonium as a gaggle of kids of all ages whooped through the house. Fancy sighed. "Welcome to the Dancer Foundation, Mr. St. Cloud. If you don't mind, why don't you go outside and walk around until we get breakfast out of the way. I'm sorry we aren't more prepared for you, but Judge Broussard caught us off guard yesterday. We've never had a live-in volunteer before so we . . . Just go outside. We'll call you after breakfast."

Jake looked at the kids who were swarming all over the place, some big, some little, some in-between. And then the dogs started barking and the cats were hissing and the kids were laughing and giggling. "If you tell me where I'm bunking, I'll take my bags there."

"Well, you see, Mr. St. Cloud, that's the problem. We don't have a place—a room for you. My mother thought . . . thinks you can sleep in one of the schoolrooms. We're going to try to find you a cot, but you might have to use a sleeping bag. And, of course, there is no shower in that building, so you'll have to do all that over here in one of our bathrooms."

"Well now, you see, Ms. Dancer, that isn't going to work for me. I require a certain amount of space, even if it is a small space. Nothing was said about accommodations other than that I may not use my own funds to improve their quality; therefore, I think I have the right to assume I'd get the equivalent space and bunk as I would have in a jail. So, before we go any further on this, you need to call someone, and I'll call my lawyer. I'm sure we can come to some kind of mutual understanding."

Fancy copped an attitude right there on the spot, her face turning beet red. "It's not like we had anything to say on the matter, Mr. St. Cloud. You were foisted on us. We did not ask for you or your help. Meaning you specifically. Furthermore, Mr. St. Cloud, I don't think you're in any position to be making demands."

Foisted? As other volunteers arrived to get the day under way, Jake bristled as he tried to control his temper. The kids were jabbering and poking each other as they jostled for the first shift at the table in the dining room. Angelica Dancer looked as if she was going to cry. Not so her daughter; Fancy Dancer looked as though she were going to chew nails and spit rust.

"Just go outside, and we'll deal with this when breakfast is over," Fancy said through clenched teeth.

Outside, Jake dropped his duffels on the

back porch. He walked down the steps and around the yard until he found a place to sit down. A second later, his cell phone was in his hand, and he was dialing Alex Rosario's number. Alex picked up on the third ring. "A problem already?"

"Yeah, and as my parole officer, I want you to take care of it. Like now, before this gets out of hand. Otherwise, I'll just go to jail. At least I'll have a bunk, a sink, and a toilet."

"Calm down and tell me what happened."

Jake rattled off his explanation.

"Okay, I'll see what I can do. You knew this wasn't going to be the Ritz."

"Yeah, well, I didn't think it was going to be cave living, either. I have rights. I want a damn bed and a bathroom. I don't mind sharing, either. And don't tell me to suck it up."

"For whatever it's worth, I agree with you, Jake. I'll see what I can do. As a last resort, I might have to go to the newspaper. Are you okay with that?"

Was he? Yes, he was okay with it. Right was right, fair was fair. "Do whatever you have to do."

As long as he had his cell phone out, he might as well follow through on his promise to call his father. Jonah St. Cloud picked up on the first ring. Jake got right to it. "What is it you wanted from me? I'm sure you have figured out by now that I'm not in a position to help anyone at the moment. But I said I would call, so I'm calling."

"You're a damn fool, Jake. I could have gotten you off. Just the way those two old fools Estes and Elroy could have gotten you off. And look what it got you."

"I noticed you didn't include Alex Rosario in your little speech. It's about accountability. I was guilty, and so I have to pay for what I did. I'm okay with it. Why can't you be okay with it? It's over and done with, so let's get on with it. What do you want from me?"

"We're having some problems on the rigs. A few spills that we contained. We have some kind of bacteria out there." He went on to talk about the water-injection systems, but Jake was only half listening. "I know you worked on that when you were in Saudi Arabia. I've been trying to call that guy you worked with, but he isn't returning my calls. I wanted you to get in touch with him. You said he was a good friend, a mentor to you. If we have another spill, it could be disastrous."

"Okay, I can do that. His field of expertise is bioremediation. If he can't help you, he can turn you on to someone who can. Does that conclude our business?"

"I'll let you know."

Jake blinked when he realized that his father had broken the connection. He shrugged; he'd done what he promised—he'd called. He had to get in touch with Tom Searles and ask him to call Jonah St. Cloud. In the end, he decided to send Tom a text rather than make a phone call. With that done, he had fulfilled his end of the bargain.

With nothing else to do, Jake sat and twiddled his fingers as he wondered how his day was going to go, since he'd gone all snarly back there in the kitchen. He looked over at what once had been a side yard but was now a parking lot of sorts. It was lined with cars. Volunteers. He mopped at his forehead with the sleeve of his shirt. It was going to be another sweltering day. Strange for September, he thought. He thought of other Septembers in the course of his life. The one that really stood out in his mind was his first year at LSU, after his mother's death. The reason it stood out was that he couldn't remember it. He shook his head to clear his thoughts. He was sick and tired of all the trips down memory lane. The past was past, and you couldn't undo it. Let it go and move on. Easier said than done.

Jake was shaken from his somber thoughts when he saw a small boy with golden curls and two missing front teeth running toward him. "Hey, Mr. Man, Miss Fancy said for me to bring you to come to the kitchen." He held his hand out to Jake, and Jake took it.

"What's your name?" Jake asked.

"Charlie."

"Okay, Charlie, let's not keep Miss Fancy waiting." They walked around the side of the house to the back porch, where Fancy Dancer was waiting for him. A peek inside the kitchen door confirmed that there was no room in the kitchen for an extra person.

Fancy took the lead. "I don't think, Mr. St. Cloud, that you are a suitable fit for us. I called the courthouse, explained our dilemma, and they're going to be sending an investigator over shortly. So, until he or she gets here, feel free to do whatever you want. Just don't get in the way of the volunteers."

Jake had a dozen snappy comebacks on his tongue, but instead of voicing them, just shrugged and walked back to where he had been sitting when young Charlie found him.

Fancy watched him go. She'd expected a few sharp-tongued retorts and was almost disappointed that she wasn't going to get the chance to debate those retorts. *Like I really need a good-looking playboy who thinks he is God's gift to women under my feet all day long. On the other hand, I've always loved a challenge. Well, too late now.*

Shortly before noon, a cavalcade of cars swerved into the parking area; some double-parked, others just parked anywhere. Jake missed the arrival because he had dozed off on the bench he was sitting on. He woke when he heard the furious shouting coming from the kitchen. He got up and ambled his way toward the back porch.

There was enough noise to rival that of a three-ring circus. He sat down on the steps and propped his elbows on his knees and listened.

"A court order is a court order."

"It doesn't matter if it's a good fit or not. You signed off on it."

"If there's no room, there's no room. I can't conjure something out of thin air."

"Then let the county fund a hotel room at night for him."

"He can't drive. Someone would have to take him there, then pick him up in the morning. This is way outside what we agreed to."

"There's no room in the budget for a year's worth of hotel rooms."

"It would take months to rescind the court order. The order stays in place."

"But I told you . . ."

"I don't care. You signed off on it. If you break the order, you will be in contempt, which in turn could lead to jail time."

"You want a full-court press on this, you got it. Where's that going to leave you and your foundation? Bad press for a place like this won't be good. You'll come across as two bitter women fighting the St. Cloud media machine."

"All right! All right! We'll clear out the attic."

"You have to be kidding. You don't have air-conditioning. The temperature in the attic would be well over a hundred degrees. That would be inhumane. Try again!"

And on and on it went. He had never in his life been the source of so much animosity. He had no idea that he had so many rights. All of which, it seemed, were being violated. He yawned and was about to doze off again when the party inside came to an abrupt halt. He jerked up just as the partygoers descended the steps and moved toward their cars. Alex, Estes, and Elroy brought up the rear, followed by a chubby little man in a wrinkled suit who turned out to be his personal advocate.

"So, am I going or staying?" Jake asked in a bored tone.

"You're staying, young man," Clarence Tremaine said firmly. "Just because you're a criminal doesn't mean anyone can strip away your rights. You will have your own room and bath. If you have even an inkling of a problem here, call me at this number," Tremaine said, handing Jake his card.

Jake didn't trust himself to speak, so he nodded.

"Well, bro, we settled that rather quickly. An hour on the job, and you had the world at your feet fighting for you. You won—how's it feel?"

"Are you being a wiseass, Alex?"

"Yeah."

"We were prepared to sue," Estes said, or maybe it was Elroy. "As soon as they realized we meant business, they backed down."

"I guess they hate me now, right?"

Alex laughed. "*Hate* might not be a strong enough word. Just let me say I wouldn't want to be in your shoes for the coming year. You got any other housekeeping chores you want me to take care of before I leave? Just bear in mind that you called me; I didn't call you."

"Bite me!" Jake growled.

"Oh dear, don't do that, Mr. Rosario. Human bites are worse than animal bites," Elroy said, or maybe it was Estes.

Jake grinned. "Thanks. Now what?"

"Now you wait for every shitty work assignment those two women can come up with, and it's yours. Do a good job now. Make me proud of you." Alex guffawed as he made his way to his car.

Estes and Elroy patted him on the back. "Don't worry, Jacob. The year will go by on winged feet."

Jake slapped at a mosquito bent on sucking out his blood. He slouched back against one of the porch pillars and waited. And waited. And then waited some more.

Finally, Fancy Dancer came out to the porch. In her hand she had a glass of frosty iced tea. She handed it over and somehow managed to spill it down the front of Jake's sweat-stained T-shirt. "Ooh, how clumsy of me. If nothing else, it should cool you off a bit. If you follow me, I'll show you to your room. I'm sorry it took so long and you had to wait, but we had to get it ready for you," Fancy said oh-so sweetly.

Jake wisely refrained from uttering a word as he followed her down a short hall, around a corner, then down a long hallway. Her face totally blank, Fancy opened the door. "I think you'll be more than comfortable here, Mr. St. Cloud." Then she turned and left.

Jake gaped. It was a huge room, with a big four-poster that was something short of regular height. The floor was bare. There wasn't a lot of clutter; in fact, there was *no* clutter. Other than a rocking chair and a large armoire, nothing else was in the room. The adjoining bathroom had a claw-foot tub with a shower curtain. Everything was old but clean. Thin yellow towels hung on a rack near the tub. He'd need at least three of them to dry off. There were no electrical outlets to be seen.

Jake was transferring his clothes to the closet and dresser when he stopped and sniffed. The faint scent of roses wafted from the drawers where he was putting his underwear and shirts. "Oh crap!" *This must be either the mother or the daughter's room.* He stopped what he was doing and ran out to the hall, shouting to Fancy.

Fancy appeared out of nowhere. "What? Doesn't the room suit you, Mr. St. Cloud?"

"Whose room is it? Yours? Your mother's? I can't take your rooms. This wasn't what I wanted. Don't you have an oversize closet or storage room I can bunk in? All I want is a real bed with four walls around me. I can't take your room."

"You're too late. The law says you get this room, so enjoy it. I hope you have nightmares every night you sleep in that bed. And for the record, it's my mother's room. She gave it up because I refused to give you my room. I was prepared for the contempt charge, but my mother wasn't. That's the bottom line. Now, you have five minutes to get down to the kitchen, so I can give you your assignment for the day."

If ever there was a time when Jake St. Cloud felt like an out-and-out shit, it was then. He watched Fancy limp her way down the long hall. He watched as twice she had to reach out to steady herself by slapping her hand against the wall.

Damn, talk about being between a rock and a hard place.

Five minutes. He hustled.

Down in the kitchen, which looked like it was getting back to normal, Jake looked around, then leaned up against the stove and waited.

Once more, Fancy Dancer appeared, seemingly out of nowhere. *She must have a light step,* he thought. He supposed that, what with being a dancer and all, she was light on her feet. There was no sign of her mother.

Fancy got right to it. "Do you know *anything at all* about kids, Mr. St. Cloud?"

"No, other than I was a kid once. Call me Jake. I think that will be easier."

"Do you know *anything* about animals?"

"No, but I always wanted a dog. It never happened."

"Today, you are going to scrub down the dog pens and the chicken coop. You will collect the eggs, wash them off, and bring them to the kitchen. Then you will patrol the yard with a pooper-scooper and clean up after the animals. There's a deposit can for the waste. You'll be in charge of that, but it will come later. We have six dogs, four cats, and a dozen chickens. You will give all the dogs a bath, dry them, then wash the towels and replace them in the locker for the next time you have to do it. The animals are crucial to the children. They're every bit as good as therapy, as animals love unconditionally."

In other words, the shit detail, Jake thought. "I thought the judge said I was to help with the kids. He didn't say anything about animals."

Fancy nibbled on her lower lip. "Do you think for one minute I'm going to turn you loose with kids when I don't even know how you're going to do with the animals? If you do think that, then think again. If you want to go whining to your legal dream team, go right ahead. Lunch is at twelve thirty. Today it's peanut butter and jelly sandwiches, apple wedges, carrot sticks, milk, and a raisin-filled cookie." Fancy turned to leave.

"What if I have a problem with the animals?"

Fancy turned, an evil smile on her face. "Then, *Jake,* I guess you're just going to have to solve it."

What she probably really means, Jake thought, *is if I'm so stupid I can't take care of an animal, for sure I do not belong here.* He supposed that was fair. And it did make sense. *Legal dream team?* Alex, Estes, and Elroy. He almost laughed out loud.

Jake sprinted down to where he knew the kennel and chicken coop were. Fresh eggs. He'd do that later. First, he had to meet the dogs and the cats. And when he did, he jumped back and said, "Whoa!" as a Doberman, a black Lab, and a Saint Bernard snapped at the chain-link fence. Two mutts and a little white fur ball sat at attention. The cats hissed and snarled as they took Jake's measure.

A young guy who turned out to be a veterinarian assistant burst out laughing. "They're always like this till they know you. The trick is to give them a treat; and whatever you do, don't show fear. Here," he said, handing over some chew treats. "Are you the new volunteer?"

Jake reached for the treats and handed them over. Tails wagged. The hissing and snarling stopped. "Yeah, I just got my marching orders. Where's the pooper-scooper?"

The young man held out his hand. "Brad Loomis."

"Jake St. Cloud. Where do I dump the. . . ?"

"Over there," Brad said, pointing to a large barrel. "Did Fancy tell you that you have to throw a shovelful of lime in the barrel each time you make a deposit?"

"No, she didn't tell me that. Got it. How much territory do I cover?"

"As far as the eye can see. The dogs like to

roam during the day. They always come back when you blow the whistle; and then you have to give up another treat."

"Okay, see you when I see you."

Brad laughed. "Yeah."

Chapter 5

Alex Rosario stopped at Starbucks, bought a latte, and instead of carrying it three doors down to his storefront law office, decided to go outside and drink it under the shade of one of the umbrellas set up on the sidewalk.

As he sipped the latte he didn't really want, he tried to make sense out of what was happening to his life since Jake St. Cloud had entered it. In just twenty-four hours, it had been turned upside down. He felt as if he'd been torn inside out and things were changing at the speed of light.

Over the years, he'd known that the day would come when he'd meet his half brother, and he had endlessly rehearsed one snide, snappy comeback after another for that inevitable meeting. He'd planned on telling him to go to hell six different ways. First in English, then in Spanish, just to make sure he got the point. The scenario he liked best was the one where they had a knock-down, drag-out fight, with Alex coming out the winner. He'd had so many preconceived notions about Jake. And he'd been wrong on all counts. How was that possible? The need to blame someone was so strong, Alex wanted to punch something until he broke his hand. Who could he blame? Certainly not his mother because, if anything, she'd been an advocate for Jake. His mother never said a bad word about anyone, not even the sperm donor. Never. Ever.

He liked Jake St. Cloud and was pretty sure Jake liked him. And now he was going to have to wait a whole year either to have a relationship with his brother or not. Maybe *relationship* was the wrong word. He tried the word *bonding* in regard to his brother. That didn't seem to quite fit, either. A brotherly *something-or-other?* No, that didn't work. He wondered what he would have done or felt if Jake hadn't stood tall and manned up in court. He would have lost respect for him, that was a given. Yet he'd been prepared to give it his all and try to get him off. *What the hell does that say about* me? The best spin he could put on it was that it was something one brother would do for another brother.

Son of a bitch! I was having a pretty good life until Jake intruded on it. Now, everything is turned upside down. Why in the damn hell am I suddenly feeling guilty?

Guilty! It made no sense. What did he have to feel guilty about? Absolutely nothing. Well, maybe over the years, when things were a little rough, he'd been a tad jealous of Jake. Just a tad, and the feeling never lasted more than a few minutes. When those feelings would surface, he'd always talk things over with his mother and his pastor, then he'd get back on track. Until the next time they wormed their way into his head.

He had a good life, a life he wouldn't trade for anything in the whole wide world. Unlike his half brother, who seemed to be searching for what Alex had. How could that be? Jake had everything. Money blowing out his ears and all the women he wanted, if he could believe what he had read in the gossip columns. Jake had a car that most guys would cut off their right arm for. He grinned when he remembered the condition of the Porsche when he'd had it towed away. Jake was an engineer with two degrees, smart as they come. He knew the oil business inside and out. He was in demand as a consultant to the big oil companies and could name his price for those consultations. He'd made his way in the world, marched to the beat of his own drum. How could he fault someone like that? As far as he was concerned, Jake had it all. Until yesterday. And even then, if he was to believe Jake, and he did, his half brother had just found out about Alex and his mother and, within the hour, was on their doorstep wanting to help them. He couldn't help but wonder, if he had been in Jake's shoes would he have done the same thing? He gave himself a mental slap to the side of his head when the answer came up *probably not.*

Alex peered into his cup. Empty. He should go to the office, but that was the last place he wanted to go. He felt as though he should be doing something. What that something was he had no clue. His mother always said when you don't know what to do, do nothing until you come up with the answer. Either you're part of the problem, or you're part of the solution. Alex shrugged and walked back inside and ordered another latte. He was back at his seat under the umbrella, taking his first sip, when he looked up to see Estes and Elroy Symon standing in front of him. Stunned, he stood, held out his hand, and motioned for the two to take a seat. He offered to get them coffee, but they politely declined.

"Do you have a few minutes, Mr. Rosario?" Elroy asked, or maybe it was Estes.

"All the time in the world. I was just sitting here trying to decide what to do about Jake or if there was anything I *could* do. What can I do for you gentlemen?"

One of the Symon brothers opened his briefcase and pulled out a thick stack of papers. He licked his finger as he flipped from page to page. "Ah, here it is. If you will just sign here on the dotted line, we can get on with business."

Suspicion ringing in his voice, Alex asked, "Sign what? I'm a lawyer, as you well know, and I never sign anything I haven't read."

"Then by all means, young man, read away," the brothers said in unison.

"Wait a minute here. It will take me all day to read through this stuff. Cut to the chase and tell me what it is. How did you find me, anyway?"

"We looked you up in the phone book, then we stopped by your office, and a young lady said we should try to find you here. Here we are. We might be old, and we might even *look* old, but we pride ourselves on being up-to-the-minute where business is concerned. What you have in your hands is Jake's mother's will. She provided for you and your mother. Of course, the names were blank until we were able to fill them in when we located you. We haven't been able to close out Selma's probate because this has been hanging over our heads since she died eighteen years ago. Now we would like to close it out. Is there a problem?"

"Well, yes, sir, there is. My mother and I don't need or want anything from the St. Cloud financial empire."

"Son, this has nothing to do with Jonah St. Cloud or St. Cloud anything. This is Jake's *mother's* estate. She was a fine, wonderful lady. I can't be sure about this, but my brother and I think she did it for Jake because she didn't ever want him to feel guilty that no one looked after you and your mother. She truly believed that one day you would surface or somehow Jake would find you on his own. Selma was always a forward-thinking woman. We also want you to know that Jake was relentless over the years in trying to find you and your mother.

"Please, don't let silly pride interfere and ruin something that is meant to be quite wonderful. You must accept the inheritance. After that, you and your mother can do whatever you want with the money. Tell me you understand everything I've just said."

Alex's head started to buzz. He didn't know what to do or say, so he just nodded.

"Then sign here, and my brother and I will walk all this over to the courthouse. We can start transferring assets and monies first thing tomorrow morning," Estes said, or maybe it was Elroy. Alex signed his name on so many papers, he thought his wrist would swell to twice its size.

"Doesn't my mother have to sign anything?"

"You have her power of attorney. We established that before we came here. We're done now, and may I say that my brother and I are more than pleased that we finally put a lid on all of this and can breathe easier. It's been a terrible responsibility weighing on us both that we couldn't honor our client's last wishes," Elroy said. This time Alex knew it was Elroy because he'd been staring at him the whole time he was speaking.

"I don't understand any of this," Alex mumbled.

"Yes, we can see that," the Symon brothers said in unison.

"We took the liberty of working up a balance sheet for you. Actually, we did three—one for Jake, one for you, and one for your mother, for easier understanding."

Alex's hand was shaking when he reached across the table for the two sheets of paper. His eye went to the bottom line. That's when he slipped off his chair and slid to the ground.

"I thought that might happen," Estes said fretfully. "We should have prepared him, Elroy."

There was no sympathy in Elroy's voice when he said, "Well, he would have fallen off the chair at that point, anyway. See, he's coming around. Help him up, Estes."

Estes reached out a bony hand and struggled to pull Alex to his feet. The three men looked at one another, and they all smiled at the same time.

Alex reached for his coffee and drained it in one long gulp as the two old lawyers packed up their worn, battered briefcases. He couldn't take his eyes off the two papers sitting in front of him. He had to fight with himself not to black out again. The two men were looking at him and saying something. He needed to listen, but it was hard to focus.

Both lawyers held out their hands. Alex extended his hand.

"Our hope is that you are the same caliber of young man Jake is. If you haven't figured it out by now, we want you to know he's a fine young man. He'll never steer you wrong. For a little while he took the wrong path, but he's back on track now. His feet are planted firmly on the ground, and he's going in the right direction. It was that promise, you see, that he couldn't fulfill no matter how hard he tried—and he did try, as we all did—that made him go off the track. What you do with your life is up to you. Give your mother our regards, young man."

"I will," Alex managed to say. "Hey, just for the record, I was doing just fine, and so was my mother, before Jake and you guys came into our lives. Yeah, we didn't have enough money for the twenty-percent down payment on that air-conditioning unit, but we managed. Just so you know."

The Symon brothers had no idea what Alex was talking about, so they just nodded sagely.

Alex watched the two lawyers walk away. His head was still spinning, so he walked back into Starbucks and ordered a straight-up black coffee. He carried it back to the table and sat down. He unfolded the papers and stared down at the numbers until his vision blurred. *Son of a gun!*

Alex burned his tongue on the coffee, but

he barely noticed. He looked down at his watch. Lunch would be almost over at Rosario's Bistro. It was just five blocks from where he was sitting. He folded the papers and jammed them into his pocket. Carrying his coffee and spilling half of it, Alex started to sprint to the bistro.

When his mother saw the expression on her son's face, she dropped a platter of pizza and ran to him.

"It's okay, Mom. Come with me, out back. I have to talk to you. *Now!*"

Sophia Rosario blindly followed her son as her help swooped in to clean up the spilled pizza and apologize to the customer, who just laughed.

"Listen, Mom, don't say anything until I'm finished. Remember now, I'm a lawyer, so what I'm telling you is true. And there's no way out. We have to accept this."

"Just tell me, Alex."

So he did. Alex was glad he had his hand on her arm, or his mother would have had the same reaction he'd had, and he told her so.

"Sixty-seven *million* dollars! And it's all ours?"

"Yes, Mom. But that's only half of it. Look at the back of the paper. That shows what we now have an interest in; that's almost a hundred million more."

Sophia closed her eyes and nearly swooned a second time. "This can't be happening to us, Alex. We didn't do anything to deserve this."

"Mom, I tried telling them that. It doesn't

matter. And Jake wanted to give it *all* to us. We can talk about it tonight when I get home. I want to go out to see Jake. I need to talk to him."

"Yes, honey, you do need to talk to your brother. Alex, does this mean I can tell my employees we can now give them health insurance and give them a bonus for their hard work and loyalty and maybe give something to Abby for her new baby, maybe help her out with her day-care bills?"

"That's what it means, Mom. It also means you can give Father John and the parish a big check for the building fund. Might be nice if you gave it in Jake's mom's name."

"Oh, you are such a smart son," Sophia said, pinching Alex's cheeks. "This isn't a dream, is it?"

"No, Mom. You do realize this is going to change our lives, don't you?"

"No, Alex, it won't. We won't let it. No, no, no. We are who we are. I will not allow anything to change our lives. Well, maybe our lives will change if you ever get married and have children. *That* is the only change I will allow. All this money will do is make things easier, but it won't change us. Go now, go see your brother and give him a hug for me."

"Now, that's over the line. Do I have to?"

Sophia cocked her head. She didn't need to do anything else.

"Okay, Mom. One hug coming up, but if he decks me, it's your fault."

Sophia laughed. Alex loved the sound; it made him think of the beach, weenie roasts, and raking leaves—all at the same time. In a word, *joyous.*

Chapter 6

It was three o'clock in the morning according to Jonah St. Cloud's spiffy Rolex watch—coincidentally, a duplicate of the one he'd seen on his son's wrist—which was sitting on the bathroom vanity. The bathroom smelled like crude oil, and he knew he'd probably clogged up the drain. As if that really mattered just then. Stark naked, water dripping from his body, he stared down at his oil-drenched clothes and work boots. Maybe he should have stripped down by the back door and left everything there to be thrown out. Too late. Too late for a lot of things. He closed his eyes. Murphy's Law. What could go wrong would go wrong. And it had, in spades.

Jonah looked in the mirror. Jesus, who the

hell was this guy staring back at him? He looked like some grizzly Neanderthal who would scare not only little children but adults as well. To shave, or not to shave the five-day growth on his face? No time to shave. He dressed quickly, knowing full well he still reeked of oil. He could have stood in the shower for hours, soaping up and rinsing off for hours on end, and he'd still smell the same. No time. That was the bottom line.

The story of his life, no time for anything but himself. No time for regrets. That's assuming he had any regrets. He really didn't. *Liar*, he chided himself.

Jonah stomped his way down the magnificent staircase, reminiscent of the one in the movie *Gone with the Wind*. Everything in the St. Cloud mansion was reminiscent of something or other. Just another way of saying *Hey, look at me and what I have. It's all about me.* The story of his life. He didn't see one damn thing wrong with that at all. You only go this way once. Life was to be enjoyed, so when those gray-black days called the aging years crept up, one could say *been there, done that, and I'd damn well do it again.* No regrets. Not one. *Liar, liar, pants on fire.*

In the kitchen, Jonah yanked open one of the cupboards and reached for a cup. He'd made coffee before he'd stumbled up the stairs to take a shower. He had to get back to the platform as soon as possible, but he had two stops to make first, middle of the night or not. He looked down at the mess he'd created when he made the coffee. He'd spilled the grounds everywhere. He was even standing in a mess of them. His housekeeper would clean it up. That's what he paid her to do, clean up after him. He gulped down the first cup of coffee, then poured another cup to take with him. He stomped his way out of the house and climbed into his monster truck. He tore down the roads, his destination Judge Porter Spindler's house on Mockingbird Court. Such a stupid name for a street, but that was Porter Spindler for you. He'd read somewhere that the judge's wife, years ago, had petitioned the authorities to change the street name because she was into bird-watching.

Jonah left the engine running in the truck when he climbed out and sprinted to the old Spindler mansion. He pressed the doorbell, keeping his thumb on it while he kicked and pounded on the massive mahogany door. Then he bellowed at the top of his lungs, "Come on, Porter, get your fat ass out of bed and open the damn door!" Finally, he saw lights go on in the mansion, then the door was being opened. Jonah shouldered his way past the overweight judge, whose sparse hair was standing on end.

"What the hell are you doing here, Jonah? It's the middle of the night, for God's sake!"

"I'm here to collect on your marker! Look, I don't have a lot of time here, so get that fat ass

of yours in gear and head for your office. I
need a subpoena and a court order rescinding
Nathan's decision regarding my son, Jake."

Judge Porter Spindler started to squawk, but
he did as Jonah said and headed for his home
office. "Just like that, you expect me to do what
you want."

"Yeah, just like that. Just you remember who
helped you when things got out of hand. You
want this whole goddamn town knowing you
have a thing for young boys? Also remember
how you got on the bench in the first place.
Now, let's make this all come out right. We
both know Nathan did what he did because he
thought he was getting back at me. That son of
a bitch deserves his Alzheimer's."

Spindler gasped. "You know about that!
How . . . ?"

"It doesn't matter how I know; I know.
That's the bottom line. Look, I wouldn't be
here if it wasn't an emergency. I need Jake out
on the platform. We have an oil spill. You read
the papers—this place revolves around oil.
Half the population works for us. Jake is to oil
what Steve Jobs was to Apple. C'mon, move it,
Porter. Give me the court order and the subpoena in case those dance ladies get huffy with
me. Let them keep the fifty grand Jake gave
them. The ankle monitor comes off ASAP, and
Jake's new probation is time spent out at the
platform, the rigs, or until I say he's no longer
needed, at which point his probation is over.

Also, while you're at it, reinstate his driver's license. Just do it, Porter."

Porter Spindler looked up at his old friend and grimaced. "We're way behind at the courthouse, so nothing has been filed yet. It's only been eight days, nine at the most—I lost count. How bad is the spill, Jonah?" he asked uneasily.

"Bad. Don't go opening your yap about this, either, or I'll be back here, and you won't like that."

"Your son has a lawyer, Jonah."

"When I leave here, you call him and set him straight. I don't want him sticking his nose in company business. You hear me, Porter? Threaten him with disbarment if he gives you any crap. We both know I can make that happen. Make sure he understands that."

"That bad, eh?" Spindler said, signing his name with a flourish and stamping the papers with his own seal. "How much oil are you losing?"

"Twenty-two thousand gallons a day. Six days now. I cut all leave, but my people have cell phones. I've heard that a few reporters are nosing around. The Coast Guard is on us like fleas on a dog. Like I said, bad."

"What the hell happened?"

"A crack. We missed it. That's all you need to know. Are we done here?"

"One thing," Spindler said, following Jonah to the front door. "How did you find out about Nathan's medical condition?"

"The same way I find out everything. I pay for information. Every damn case that came before him in the last ten years will be suspect if word gets out. So, Porter, be very careful what you say and do from here on in. Do we understand each other?"

"We do, Jonah. I'll make sure everything is contained, so there will be no blowback."

"See that you do," Jonah said as he walked off into the night.

Thirty minutes later, Jonah St. Cloud was ringing the doorbell of the Dancer plantation house. He thought about kicking the door the way he had at Spindler's but decided to wait. Lights went on almost immediately. He could see a young woman running to the front door. She opened it, her eyes wild with fright. "Please, stop ringing the doorbell. You'll wake all the children. What is it? What do you want?"

"Where's Jake St. Cloud? He's supposed to be here."

"He is . . . was, but he refused to take my mother's room after that fiasco when he first showed up. He's sleeping in the schoolroom. Why? What has he done *now*?"

"He hasn't done anything, you stupid female. When something goes wrong, why do you women immediately think any male in the vicinity is automatically the culprit? Here, this is for your reading pleasure. Where is the damn schoolroom?"

Fancy scanned the papers she was holding. Her hands started to shake. "I don't understand any of this."

"Ask me if I care, lady. Now, where is the schoolroom? This is the second time I'm asking you. If I ask you a third time, I will have this place shut down in the blink of an eye," Jonah threatened. He was pleased at the fear he saw in the young woman's eyes. He just dearly loved putting the fear of God into people. Simply because he could. Jonah St. Cloud was every bit the nasty character Jake had him pegged to be.

Fancy turned when she heard the soft whir of her mother's wheelchair.

"What's going on, Fancy?"

Fancy straightened her shoulders. "Mr. St. Cloud has just served papers on us—a subpoena and a court order. It seems he will be taking Jake, his son, with him, and Jake will no longer be doing his probation service with us. All of that has been done away with."

"Don't you mean slavery?" Jonah barked.

"At four o'clock in the morning?" Angelica Dancer exclaimed.

"Yes, at four o'clock in the morning," Jonah said. "That should give you some idea that this is not fun and games. Now, where the hell is the schoolroom? If I have to ask you again, I will have the entire police force here within ten minutes to carry through on my threat."

"Show him, Fancy, so that this rich, rude, obnoxious oaf leaves our house and never returns."

Jonah was tempted to let loose with a tirade but thought better of it. He followed Fancy, who was running through the house in her pajamas and bare feet, turning on lights, her long mane of dark hair flying out behind her.

Outside, she paused to catch her breath and pointed to the building at the far end of the path. The dogs, sensing something out of the norm, started to bark. When the floodlights came on, the two roosters in the chicken coop started to crow.

"This place is a nuthouse," Jonah grumbled as he loped along behind Fancy.

"And, of course, you're the biggest nut of all, is that what you're trying *not* to say?" Fancy said boldly. At the door to the schoolroom, Fancy opened it and called out, "Mr. St. Cloud, there's someone here to see you."

A light went on. Fancy flinched when she saw Jake roll off the skimpy cot that, along with his sleeping bag, he used for a bed.

"Get dressed, son. You're coming with me!" Jonah said.

Jake was instantly wide-awake. *Jesus, am I having a nightmare?* "Like hell I am. I can't leave here. I'm on probation. I don't have to do what you say, you vicious old man. Why are you terrorizing these people?"

Fancy held out the papers Jonah had given

her up at the house. "I'm afraid you have to do what he says, Jake."

Jake looked at the young woman in her pajamas and bare feet. She'd just called him Jake. Until then, it had been "Hey you," or "*Mister* St. Cloud." She'd almost belted him when he absolutely refused to move into her mother's bedroom. She'd tried offering her own room, but he'd refused that, too. While he didn't like sleeping on a flimsy cot with a sleeping bag, he was doing it, all the while cursing that corrupt judge's ban on using his own money to upgrade his accommodations. At the end of the day, he was more tired working at the Dancer Foundation than he had been when he used to work on the oil rigs. He reached for the papers she was holding out to him. He scanned them, then looked up at his father. "You really are a son of a bitch, you know that!"

"Save the endearments for later, Jake. Get dressed. I'll cut that monitor off you when you get in the truck. And your driver's license has been reinstated."

Jake didn't move. He looked at Fancy and said, "Will you please call my attorney? His name is Alex Rosario. I'm not going anywhere until he gets here."

"Won't do you any good. His wings have been clipped. Get dressed, Jake. You want him to lose his license to practice law? Keep this shit up, and it will happen. I will make it happen. I'm waiting, son."

Jake took a deep breath and held it. He wondered if he would turn blue if he held it long enough. He finally expelled it when his father tossed him his clothes. He was beaten, and he knew it.

Outside, in the early-morning air, Jake looked at Fancy and said, "I apologize for my father's boorish behavior." He couldn't be sure, but he thought he saw tears in her eyes. He turned away and climbed into the truck. His thoughts were everywhere as his father went to work on the ankle monitor with a box cutter. He watched it sail off into the darkness. He knew one of the dogs would find it and probably chew it to pieces.

"So, it happened, didn't it? I warned you three years ago to take care of that crack. How much oil is leaking out?"

"Somewhere in the neighborhood of twenty-two thousand gallons a day."

"That means around thirty thousand. We both know that you don't know how to tell the truth. You're never going to learn, are you? You're way past due for an explosion."

"Well, wonder boy, you're going to fix all that now, aren't you?" Jonah snarled.

Jake wisely kept silent. All he could really think about was the awful look on Fancy Dancer's face and how the scar on her face looked in the moonlight.

Back at the house, Fancy limped her way up the back steps to the back porch and on into the kitchen, where her mother was making coffee. "What happened, Fancy?"

"I don't know, but whatever it is, it must be serious because Jake went with him. He told me at first to call his lawyer. And then his father said not to bother, that his wings had been clipped. I take that to mean whatever the attorney would try to do wouldn't work. I saw on the news a couple of days ago that Judge Porter Spindler is now the St. Tammany Parish judge. He's the one who signed those papers at three o'clock in the morning. Favors called in. Blackmail. Something, Mom. I'm going to call that lawyer anyway."

"Honey, it's four twenty in the morning. Wait at least until six."

"We're not sleeping, so why should he sleep? He left his card, Mom. Do you know where I put it?"

"In the kitchen drawer where you throw all your junk. Are you sure that's a good idea?"

"Probably not, but I'm going to do it anyway." And she did. When she heard the sleepy voice on the other end of the phone, she shrilled, "Wake up, Mr. Rosario, your client asked me to call you."

"What client? Who is this? Do you know what time it is?"

"Your client, Jake St. Cloud. This is Fancy Dancer, and it is exactly four twenty-two. Are you sufficiently awake to hear me out?"

"Spit it out! What did he do *now?*"

"He didn't do anything. It's his father." She quickly related what had just transpired. "He went with his father."

"Well, we'll just see about that!"

"His father said your wings had been clipped. I take that to mean anything you try to do for your client will be ineffectual."

"And the judge was who?"

"Judge Porter Spindler."

"Oh shit! Okay, I'm getting dressed. I'll be out there in thirty minutes. You still have the papers, right?"

"I still have them. Jake threw them on the floor when his father showed them to him. I guess I'll see you when I see you."

The connection broken, Fancy turned to her mother. "He's coming out here."

"Company at four thirty in the morning! What is this world coming to? I think we should get dressed, don't you, Fancy?" Angel said, a smile playing around the corners of her mouth.

"I guess so. Do you need help, Mom?"

"No. I'm good. Run along, dear. I want some coffee first."

When Fancy left the kitchen, Angelica Dancer maneuvered her wheelchair so that she had easy access to the counter on which the coffeepot rested. She poured with trembling hands. Lord, she hated how crippled she'd become. It wouldn't be long now before her hands would betray her, and she'd have to eat foods she could grasp in both hands. She could walk, and at times she did, but the pain was so excruciating, she opted for the chair most of the time. She struggled to put on what she called her game face as she stared off into space.

She worried about her daughter just the way any mother would worry about her child. Fancy was . . . bitter. She was also angry. She cried at night, and Angelica knew this because her room was right next to Fancy's. She herself had gone through all the emotions her daughter was going through. But somewhere along the way she'd lost the anger and the bitterness because she knew it wasn't healthy to harbor such hatred. *Fancy*, she told herself, *just isn't at that point yet.*

The moment she'd set eyes on Jake St. Cloud, her thoughts had whizzed forward like a freight train out of control. Maybe he was *the one* for Fancy. She'd seen the gentleness in his eyes and knew somehow that he was a kind man. When she'd relayed her observations about Jake to her daughter, Fancy had reared back and spewed all kinds of things about his being a rich, no-account playboy, a selfish individual who thought the law didn't apply to him. Then she'd said, *Did you see that Rolex on his wrist? Well, let me tell you how much that cost. That watch goes for over a hundred thousand dollars. I just saw a picture of it in one of those magazines we get. We could run this place for two years on what he squandered on a stupid watch.* Angel had been appalled at the venom in her daughter's voice and dropped the issue of Jake St. Cloud.

Angel's eyes filled with tears. How many hours had she spent in the beginning, listening to her daughter during the long nights as she tried unsuccessfully to work the ballet bar because she was determined to dance again. It was so heartbreaking to listen through the walls or outside the door as she would stumble and fall only to get up and stumble and fall again until her body was black-and-blue. Even then, she hadn't given up. The night she'd fractured her hip and had to be transported to the hospital by the EMTs was when she gave up. When the orthopedic specialists had told her that arthritis would set in at some point and raised the possibility she could end up like her mother, that was all she finally needed to give up her dream of being a prima ballerina. At her suggestion that Fancy talk to a therapist, her daughter had gone ballistic, saying she didn't need to talk to anyone. They never spoke of it again.

It was strange to Angel that the scar on Fancy's face didn't seem to bother her. She wasn't vain, never had been, even as a young girl. Beauty, she'd said, was in the eye of the beholder. And yet, she had seen Fancy's hand go to her face in a reflexive motion when Jake St. Cloud entered their lives ever so briefly. The very next day, Fancy had loosened her hair so that it draped over her cheek whenever she felt the need to hide the scar.

Angel sighed as she set her coffee cup on the counter and wheeled herself out of the room and down the hall to her own room. All she could do was pray that her daughter would come to terms with her capabilities and deal with them in a rational manner. Nine years was just way too long to wallow in self-pity. Just way too long.

Chapter 7

Alex Rosario threw on an old pair of sweats and a tattered workout shirt. His feet went into equally battered sneakers. He didn't bother to tie the laces. He galloped through the house and ran smack into his mother in the kitchen. Startled, she backed up and stared at her son. "Do you know what time it is? Where are you going at this hour of the morning, Alex? Is something wrong?" she asked anxiously.

"Miss Dancer called me and said that the court terminated Jake's probation at the foundation, and he had to leave the premises. With his father. She seemed very upset. She wants me to see the court papers. I guess she couldn't sleep and decided to call me. I don't know, Mom, but that's why I'm going there."

"I guess that makes sense. Call me if there's anything I can do."

"I will, Mom." Alex gave his mother a bone-crushing hug and ran out to his car.

With no traffic on the road, Alex arrived at the Dancer home in twenty-three minutes. Lights outside and on the first floor blazed in the darkness. He drove around to the back of the property, near the rear entrance, and parked his car. Fancy Dancer was standing in the doorway. He could see her mother in her wheelchair behind her. *Why does crap always happen to nice people?*

When no answer was forthcoming, Alex bounded up the steps. Angelica Dancer held out a cup of coffee. He reached for it gratefully. Out of the corner of his eye, he saw two pieces of paper on the kitchen table.

"Jake just left with him? Did he say anything?"

Fancy shook her head. "Well, yes, he did. He apologized to me for his father's obnoxious behavior. He was angry at his father, I can tell you that. He did not want to go with him."

"But he went, that's the bottom line." Alex reached for the papers on the table and read through them. Then he threw his hands in the air. "I don't think there's anything I can do. I'm willing to try but . . ."

"Jake said to call you. I assume that means he wants you to try," Fancy said as she kneaded her hands together. "What will happen to you if you try?"

Alex shrugged. "Sometimes you just can't fight the politics of a small town. Judge Spindler is a crony of Jonah St. Cloud's. Everyone within a hundred-mile radius of Slidell knows that oil controls everything around here. You say the word *oil*, and in the next breath the name *Jonah St. Cloud* pops out of your mouth. No one is going to go up against *that*. This is a wild guess on my part, but something serious must have happened on the rig for the old man to call in markers and spring Jake like that."

"Jake wasn't happy to be going with his father. He was doing very well here. He didn't cause one bit of trouble, and he did everything we told him to do plus a little extra. The kids liked him, and it appeared to us that he liked them." This last was said so grudgingly that Alex stared at Fancy in disbelief.

Fancy turned defensive. "I had . . . what I mean is . . ."

"What my daughter is trying to say is that she had preconceived ideas about Jake, owing to the press coverage he's had over the years. The young man who reported in to us is nothing like what we read about him. He didn't expect anything; nor did he ask for anything. He refused to take my room, and when my daughter offered hers, he refused that, too, and even apologized for creating a fuss on the day of his arrival. He's been sleeping on a rickety cot with a sleeping bag and showering up here at the house. To me, that says a lot about that young man."

"So now you're shorthanded with Jake gone?"

"We'll get by. We did before he came. Each time we have the newspapers run a story on us, we get a new wave of volunteers. We have it under control, at least for now," Fancy said.

"This is just my opinion, but only a fool would have turned down whatever Mr. St. Cloud's offer was. I'm thinking it was some kind of oil emergency, and when that's over and done with, Jake is a free agent. Staying here, he was locked into a full year with that ankle monitor and loss of his driving privileges. I'm being honest here. I would have done the same thing," Angel said.

"Mom, Jake didn't want to go with his father. He had no choice," Fancy snapped. "You saw him; you heard him; he wasn't thinking long-term. He didn't want to go, period."

Alex thought Fancy was sounding more agitated by the moment. Maybe *agitated* was the wrong word. Maybe *frustrated* was the word he was looking for. The question at the moment, though, was why would she be expressing either emotion, considering her initial reaction to Jake? Definitely something to think about when he had more time. At present, though, he had to get home and get showered and changed so he could head to the courthouse to see what he could do for Jake. If anything.

Alex folded the papers and jammed them

into the pocket of his sweatpants. "I don't know what, if anything, I can do, but I'm more than willing to take a shot at doing something. Jake didn't say what he wanted me to do, did he?"

"No, just to call you," Fancy said. "Will you let us know what happens?"

"Of course. Sorry you got your night's sleep ruined."

"Sleep? What's that?" Angel smiled. "It's not something to worry about, young man."

"Well then, I guess I'd better get going, because I'll have to go into the office first. I'll call you when I know something."

Fancy walked Alex to the door. "Thank you for coming out, Mr. Rosario. I'm sorry about all of this. For whatever this is worth, Jake did not want to go with his father. I couldn't hear what they were saying, but I could tell that Jake was very angry with that man when they left the house. Parents and their children should not be adversaries, and that's what it looked like to me from where I was standing. My mother thought the same thing."

Alex nodded. Not for all the oil in the Gulf of Mexico would he divulge Jake's feelings about his father to this young woman and her mother. He simply nodded and left the house.

It was still dark out as Alex drove home. His mother had probably left already for the restaurant. He felt a pang of guilt that she had to go to work so early in the morning, when it was still dark out, to get ready for the breakfast crowd. He felt a new appreciation for his mother.

There was a little more traffic on his return than when he had left. The early birds who had to be at work by six were on the road and looking for a place to stop to fuel up on coffee before starting the daily grind.

Fifteen minutes later, Alex was sprinting from his car to the back door. He smiled when he saw that his mother had left the porch light on for him. Once inside, he turned it off, a rule of his mother's. *We do not live to make the electric company happy.* Translation: turn off the lights when you leave a room. After long years of practice, it was an ingrained habit.

The kitchen smelled good. His mother had baked him some cinnamon buns. They were still warm. The coffeemaker was ready—he just had to press the button.

Alex sat down at the table to wait for the coffee to drip into the pot. Damnation, he needed to think. *Think!* What was it Jake expected him to do? More to the point, what *could* he do? Obviously, Jake thought that there was something he could do; otherwise he would not have told Fancy Dancer to call him. What? He wasn't a high-dollar attorney people listened to. He was a simple storefront lawyer who would never get rich practicing his kind of law. A month ago, he'd thought about moonlighting just to get a little ahead, so he could have a cushion if he fell on hard times.

Alex was off his chair the moment he heard the last gurgle of coffee dripping into the pot.

He barely noticed that he'd scalded his tongue or even how tasty the cinnamon buns were, because his head was buzzing like an angry beehive. He needed a diversion. He turned on the small television set his mother kept on the kitchen counter so that before she went to bed she could watch the soaps she was addicted to. He suffered through the weather report—overcast and cloudy with the temperatures in the low sixties. To him, the low sixties was shiver weather. He tucked the thought into his mind to dress accordingly, as the heating system in the storefront was less than desirable.

The weather guy drifted off, and the early-morning newsperson, makeup intact, his hair blow-dried, appeared, his expression solemn as he said, *"While this has not been one-hundred-percent confirmed, reliable sources are telling us that there's been an oil spill at the St. Cloud oil rig."* Mr. Pretty Boy News Anchor looked down at what Alex presumed was a monitor of some sort, and said, *"This is just coming in now, and, again, not confirmed, that Jake St. Cloud, the son of Jonah St. Cloud, has been seen going out to the rig. The only reason this could be happening, I'm told by a source, is that there is, indeed, an oil spill. We have calls in to the Coast Guard, but so far nothing has been confirmed from them, either."*

Alex felt his stomach clench into a tight

knot. He remembered only too well how the BP oil explosion and the disaster that followed had hurt the people and the state of Louisiana and the whole Gulf region. He'd heard back then, when the rumblings were so fierce, that Jake had been called in months earlier and had warned the oil company of an imminent explosion. He hadn't paid that much attention at the time because Jake St. Cloud was on his shit list, right up there in the number one spot. Now, he *had* to pay attention.

Alex continued to gulp at his coffee, getting up to refill his cup. He looked down at the tray of cinnamon buns and realized he'd eaten six of them, which meant he was going to have to run ten miles instead of five after work. He continued to listen as the news anchor started rehashing all the things that had gone wrong with BP and pointing fingers and making veiled accusations.

Alex turned off the coffeemaker and wrapped the remaining sticky buns in plastic wrap. Satisfied that the kitchen was tidy, he rinsed his cup and put it in the dishwasher before sprinting up the stairs to take his morning shower.

Forty minutes later, Alex locked the door and headed for his car. His watch said that it was six forty-five. Fifteen more minutes and he'd have hit rush-hour traffic. By leaving at this time, he'd make it to the office at exactly seven o'clock if he hit every traffic light just right. If not, he'd be strolling into his office at ten after. Time to do what he had to do to get

ready for his day, then head off to the courthouse to get his body pounded into the
ground by some damn cranky judge who was
probably on Jonah St. Cloud's payroll.

At precisely three minutes to eight, Alex
Rosario walked through the courthouse doors
and stood patiently behind a long line of
lawyers, defendants, and plaintiffs waiting to
go through security. When it was his turn, he
plopped his briefcase down and emptied his
pockets. "No, I don't have a cell phone on
me," he said to one of the security guards.

On the other side of the scanner, Alex pock-
eted his keys and loose change and swept his
briefcase off the conveyor belt. He strode
down the hall in search of the court clerk's office, where he planned to ask for a ten-minute
meeting with St. Tammany Parish Judge Porter
Spindler. In the world of the law, ten minutes
was a lifetime, or so judges would have you believe.

Alex slowed down as he approached the
clerk's office. He looked around and wondered if all courthouses looked like this one.
He'd never tried a case, because he wasn't a lit-
igator. While he was no stranger to this particular courthouse, he wasn't all that familiar
with it, either. He'd appeared before judges on
behalf of his clients and taken his prizes and
his lumps like every other lawyer walking
around the halls. He sniffed and thought
about the different schools he'd attended and
how they all smelled the same, of chalk and

paper and that green stuff the janitors poured on the floor, whatever it was called. Every day was the same—the smell had never intensified nor lessened all during his school years. The courthouse was the same way, but he couldn't identify this smell, and it bothered him. He was just being nervous, he told himself, because he knew that if Spindler agreed to see him, the judge would smack him down hard. First rule: never argue with a judge unless you want contempt charges filed against you. The other unwritten rule was you sucked it up, you smiled, then you headed to the men's room to lick your wounds. *Well, that damn well isn't going to happen. Not today.*

Alex opened the door to the clerk's office to see a dour-looking woman with glasses perched on the end of her nose. Just eight o'clock, and she already looked like she'd eaten two lawyers for breakfast and spit out two others. She looked up at Alex and said, "Speak!"

"I'm Alex Rosario. I represent Jake St. Cloud. I need to speak with Judge Spindler as soon as possible. It's important, or I wouldn't be here," Alex said as forcefully as he could.

Maybe it was the name St. Cloud, maybe it was his own good looks, or maybe the dragon in the clerk had a soft spot, because she eyed him a moment longer, told him to sit down, and said she'd be right back. Before she opened the door, she asked, "How much time do you need, Mr. Rosario, assuming Judge Spindler has some free time?"

Alex almost swallowed his tongue. "Ten minutes! Five if I talk fast."

A small smile stretched across the dragon's face. "Five might work."

Alex felt as though there were an army of ants crawling around inside his stomach as he waited for the clerk to return. When she did, he was relieved to see the smile on her face. "The judge said he can see you right now for *five* minutes. When he says *five minutes,* he means *five* minutes. Do you understand that, Mr. Rosario?"

"I do, ma'am, and thank you." This was just too damn easy. It had to be the St. Cloud name. *Five minutes. Crap, it will take that long to get my tongue to work.*

"I'm waiting, Mr. Rosario," the clerk snapped. "Follow me, please. And let me warn you ahead of time, the judge does not appear to be in a good mood this morning."

"Neither am I, ma'am," Alex said boldly. "Neither am I." He repeated the words more for himself than the court clerk.

Chapter 8

It was the first time Alex had ever been in a judge's chambers. He looked around and admitted to himself that he was impressed: dark paneling on the walls polished to a high sheen; the one-of-a-kind coatrack where the judge's robe hung on a padded hanger; pictures on the wall, of the judge and the governor, the judge and the vice president of the United States, the judge and the secretary of state, the judge and everyone and anyone. On the shelf behind his massive desk were pictures that appeared to be of family, all in the same kind of ornate frames. Two easy chairs sat nestled across the room, with a small table in front of them, legal magazines stacked neatly upon it. A lush green ficus tree looked so perfect as it reached toward the overhead fluorescent lighting that Alex wondered if it was real. He was tempted to pinch one of the leaves but then remembered why he was here.

"Thank you for seeing me on such short notice, Judge Spindler. I appreciate it."

Spindler leaned across the antique-looking desk, and asked, "What can I do for you so early in the morning, Counselor?"

Alex eyed Spindler and wondered why he wasn't feeling intimidated. He looked just like any other old, cranky judge who should have retired years ago. The court system needed new blood, younger blood. If he didn't know it before, he knew it now for sure. It wasn't just his opinion, either. He'd heard his colleagues moaning and groaning about the ancient old men who ran the courthouse.

The judge looked tired, as if he hadn't slept. Then again, maybe it was the harsh overhead lighting. "I'm here about a client of mine, Jake St. Cloud. I want someone to tell me why his probation at the Dancer Foundation was terminated, and I also want to know where he is. As the attorney of record and his court-appointed probation officer, I should have been notified as to any changes and his current whereabouts."

"Well, Counselor, it's like this. Judge Broussard made a serious mistake. As much as I hate to have to admit this, he made a grievous error in Mr. St. Cloud's sentencing. It was caught in time and has since been rectified. For the betterment of Mr. St. Cloud, I might say."

"Would Mr. St. Cloud be Jonah St. Cloud, Your Honor, or Jake St. Cloud, Jonah's son and my client?"

"What kind of question is that, Mr. . . . what was your name again?"

"Rosario, Judge. Alex Rosario. It's the kind of question that requires an answer. A judge's rescinding a previous sentence at three o'clock in the morning raises questions that I would like answered. In other words, Judge, I don't believe what you're telling me. If I don't get a satisfactory response from you, I will feel duty-bound to go to the media to protect my client. In case you don't know this, my client was satisfied with his sentence and was serving it to the best of his ability. I want you, Your Honor, to tell me why Jonah St. Cloud, my client's father, was able to go to the Dancer residence and take my client away at around four o'clock this morning. Jonah St. Cloud is not an officer of this court. Nor was he my client's probation officer. I was, and still am, unless something not in the documents presented to my client says otherwise."

"Are you questioning my judgment, young man?"

"Well, Your Honor, I guess I am. I want answers, and I want them now. I have a client I've sworn to represent to the best of my ability because I am an officer of the court, as you are. That's why I'm here."

Spindler's voice turned testy, and Alex noticed

the tremor in the judge's hands that hadn't been apparent seven minutes ago. And there was something in his eyes . . . a spark of . . . was it anger, or was it fear? Whatever he thought he was seeing, Alex knew it didn't bode well for him or his brand-new client.

"You've used up more than the five minutes I agreed on. I gave you my answer. This court moved to rectify a ruling that was not only unjust but unfair, rendered by a sick judge who had no right to be ruling on any matters in his condition. Now, what part of that don't you understand, Counselor?"

Alex squared his shoulders. He felt a little like David going into the lion's den with just a business card and a ballpoint pen when the man sitting in front of him had an AK-47 locked and loaded, or whatever the saying was. Maybe he was not kowtowing to the judge because he now had money in the bank; money that would take care of him, his mother, and any wife and children he had for the rest of their lives.

But that wasn't totally it, he knew. He hated injustice, and he hated the good-old-boy network that ran that courthouse. His gut told him to keep pressing.

"The part about Jonah St. Cloud's getting you to sign off on those papers at three o'clock in the morning, then whisking my client off to God knows where—that's the part I don't understand, Judge. To the best of my recollection, we don't do things like that in Louisiana in the middle of the night. Those are Gestapo tactics, which I learned about in school."

The old judge flinched at Alex's words. He stood up. "We're done here, Counselor. I have to take the bench."

"I understand, Judge Spindler. Make sure you set aside some time today to talk to the media, because that's where I'm going when I leave."

"That sounds like a threat to me. Is it a threat, Mr. Rosary?"

"Rosario, Your Honor. My name is Rosario. Alex Rosario. No, it wasn't a threat. It was a statement of fact. Thank you, Judge Spindler, for taking the time to bullshit me this morning."

The judge stood and walked over to retrieve his judge's robe. "How dare you! How dare you speak to a sitting judge in such a manner! I could have you arrested for contempt right now."

Alex was pleased to see that the judge's hands were shaking so badly, he couldn't get his robe off the hanger. Alex removed it for him. The fortune that was now in his bank account gave him the courage to respond. "Then do it, Your Honor. If nothing else, it will speed things up."

They were the same height, eyeball to eyeball, Alex noticed, but the judge's shoulders were bowed.

"I used the word *could*, Counselor. I have no

desire to ruin your career when you're just starting out. I'm more than willing to overlook your disrespect of me. I have to ask myself why you would want to ruin my career at this stage of the game."

"It's not a *game*, Judge. Such an odd choice of words from a sitting judge. But to answer your question: because I think you're beholden somehow, some way, to Jonah St. Cloud. It's you who is ruining the end of your own career, a career that I might say up until now has been distinguished. Why are you protecting Jonah St. Cloud? What do you owe him? Or is he holding something over your head that you aren't real proud of? I think you need to ask yourself if Jonah St. Cloud would do the same for you. I'm not a betting man, but I don't think he would. I think that he would gladly let you swing in the wind as long as he gets what he wants."

Porter Spindler raised his head and looked into Alex's eyes. He saw only determination, and he knew right then that the young lawyer would keep his word and go to the media. And that would be the end of him. He'd be no better off than Nathan Broussard. Although, unlike Nathan, he still had his mind.

The judge walked back to his desk and sat down. He motioned for Alex to come forward. "Everything I told you about Judge Broussard was the truth. He and Jonah St. Cloud have a bad history, and I'm sure that influenced his ruling to a certain extent. Having said that, I wasn't aware of that particular ruling until Jonah apprised me of it. It was over the top and needed to be rescinded. Anyone could fill Jacob's shoes at the Dancer Foundation home. But no one could or can fill Jake St. Cloud's shoes at the oil platform. There's been an oil spill that Jonah has been trying to keep under wraps. He needed Jake. Jake knows how to use bacteria to eat up the spill or something like that. I just know it's serious and Jonah didn't want the people to panic and he sure as hell didn't want another disaster like BP's. That's it in a nutshell."

Alex digested what he was being told. At least it made sense. "Jake didn't want to go."

"I suppose not. It's no secret that Jake and his father have a very acrimonious relationship that goes back years and years. In the end, I'm sure he went along with it not because of his father but because it was the right thing to do."

Alex knew in his gut that the judge was right. "I want to talk to my client," he said forcefully.

"Well, young man, I certainly can't stop you from doing that, but I seriously doubt you'll get anywhere near that platform."

"Then I want you to call Jonah St. Cloud and tell him to make Jake available to me by phone. I know Jake doesn't have a cell phone with him, because he left it behind at the Dancer house. Tell him if I don't hear from Jake in the next few hours, I *will* go to the media. Call it a reprieve, Your Honor."

The old judge's shoulders sagged. "All right, I'll try to reach him. Give me your cell-phone number, and I'll be in touch." Alex scribbled the number on the back of his business card before he handed it over to the judge.

The judge's clerk knocked and opened the door. "They're waiting, Your Honor," she said briskly.

"Let them wait a little longer. I'll be out when I'm ready." The clerk withdrew.

Alex turned to leave.

"Mr. Rosario, I respect your tenacity."

Alex turned around and later wondered where the words came from. "You ain't seen nothing yet, Judge. I'm just warming up."

Alex was a whirlwind as he flew out the door, down the hall, and out of the courthouse, where, the moment he stepped onto the parking lot, he raised his fist and shouted, "Way to go, Alex!" He didn't care who saw him or what they thought of his little performance. *Yessiree, a lot of money in the bank is one of the most powerful aphrodisiacs in the world. Yessiree!*

And he owed it all to his half brother, Jake.

Chapter 9

Jake St. Cloud stared off into the distance, his thoughts miles away. He was jerked back to the reality of his situation when Zeke Anders, foreman on the platform, clapped him on the back. Zeke was a grizzled old oilman who should have retired years before, but the oil business was in his blood and the only thing he knew. Plus he spent his money faster than he made it, and, if you were to believe him, he didn't have a pot to piss in. Which, Jake thought, was probably true if he believed the tales he'd heard over the years. He liked Zeke, and Zeke was the one who had encouraged him during his teen years of forced labor on the rigs to go to college to make something of himself. *Otherwise,* he'd said ominously, *you're going to end up like me.* Jake had been grateful to

Zeke for the way he'd taken him under his wing and watched over him like a doting grandmother, and he had acquired two degrees in engineering; his biomedical engineering degree was why he was standing on that platform. It was why his expertise was sought after by just about every oil company in the world.

Zeke clapped Jake on the back again and said, "Where's the old man?"

"Who cares?" Jake snapped.

"That bad, eh?"

Jake didn't bother to answer.

"When we lock this down and put this puppy to bed, I'm outta here. I wanted you to be the first to know. Some of the others are going with me, too," Zeke said through clenched teeth. "I've always been square with you, kid."

"I know that, Zeke. Does *he* know? Where will you go? What will you do?" Jake was alarmed at Zeke's statement but didn't know why.

Zeke laughed. "Figured I'd find me some shack or lean-to and hang up my spurs. Not that I wear spurs, mind you, just a figure of speech. I'll stare off into the sunset and tell myself I had a hell of a good run. I'll have my pension and social security, which should take me through the first five days of the month, maybe seven if I'm frugal. And then I'll just hope that someone takes pity on me and helps me out the other twenty-five days until the old pension rolls in again at the first of the next month."

Alex stared down at the thick, oily water. "Kind of risky, Zeke, don't you think?"

"Kid, life is all about risk one way or the other. Like I said, I had a hell of a run, and I'd do it all over again the exact same way if I had the chance. Been awhile, boy. What's going on with you? These bacteria are gonna work, aren't they, Jake?"

"Not much. Same old, same old," Jake said shortly. "I think so. No reason to believe they won't, since I've used them before in the Middle East. Can I use your cell phone, Zeke? I left in such a hurry, I forgot to bring mine with me."

Zeke dug down into his greasy, oil-slicked coveralls and pulled out a state-of-the-art cell phone Jake knew did everything but cook breakfast. His eyebrows shot up as he looked down at the phone, his eyes full of questions. "Gotta stay in touch with my ladies. You know how it is."

Jake shook off his greasy glove and sent off a text message to Alex Rosario. He thanked God he even remembered the number. No sooner had he sent it off than he looked up to see his father coming toward him. He had a cell phone in his hand, which he held out to Jake. "Your lawyer wants to talk to you." He handed over the phone to Jake, then turned to Zeke. "You got nothing better to do than stand here and jaw with Jake, Zeke?"

Zeke rubbed one of his rough, callused hands over the whiskers on his face. All he succeeded in doing was to smear the black oil to the other side of his face. He glared at his boss but didn't say anything before he sauntered off.

Jake turned his back to his father and brought the phone up to his ear. "Yeah, it's me, Jake. Talk to me, buddy." Jake listened, then said, "I just sent you a text. Get back to me on it. Same number, yeah."

Jake handed the phone back to his father. "Wheeling and dealing the way you always do. How's that working for you, *Dad*?"

"Let me worry about how it's all working for me. Just do your job, and we'll call it a day. You should be thanking me for getting you out of that shit-hole Broussard sent you to. If you're telling the truth about the bacteria and they work, you'll have paid your debt to society in the next ten days or so. And then you'll be free as the breeze, *son*."

Jake ignored his father's words and looked up at the sky. Black clouds were scudding overhead so fast, he was getting dizzy just looking at them. He could already feel the heavy moisture in the air. Rain? Without a doubt. Storm? Absolutely. Not good. Not good at all. He moved away on the oil-slicked platform, anything to get away from the hateful man standing there glaring at his back.

Back in town, Alex tried to make sense of the text from Jake. *Do what you have to do.* Well, fine, he'd do that as soon as he figured out whatever the hell *that* was. Truth be told, he was surprised his sperm donor had even answered the phone, much less put Jake on. Obviously, Judge Spindler had gotten to Jonah, and the sperm donor was going to keep it all close to the vest. Did Jake mean *go to the media?* What would that do, other than cause a panic? Still, didn't the people have a right to know what was going on in their waterways? He thought then about how much fish he ate and how much fish his mother served at the restaurant. His mind whirled with all the horror stories after the BP fiasco, with everyone blaming everyone else, nothing getting done, and the impact on the entire Gulf region.

Alex looked down at the rest of the text. Now, *that* he understood. *That* he could handle. First things first, though. Without stopping to think, he called the *Times-Picayune* and unloaded. Then he called the Coast Guard and asked questions and demanded answers. Not that he got any. His third call was to the Symon brothers; he spoke to Elroy, or maybe it was Estes. He outlined his plan, waited for approval, and almost cheered when he got it: "As Jake's lawyers, if that's what he wants, then that's good enough for Estes and me." Aha, it was Elroy. He was getting good at distinguishing which brother was which. Yeah, right.

* * *

Alex felt proud of himself at the storm he'd created, as one day led into the next, until five long weeks had gone by, with the nation watching Jake St. Cloud work what the media were calling a miracle of sorts.

It was the middle of October when Alex turned on the TV in his small, cramped office and heard the morning commentator announce that Jake St. Cloud would be leaving the platform and heading home. They showed an aerial shot of Jake, taken by a news group from a helicopter. He leaned forward for a better look. He didn't think he'd ever seen anyone more ragged, more filthy, in his life. His brother.

Well, hot damn! His fist shot in the air in victory. He thought about letting out a war whoop, but his partners had clients down the hall. Instead, he packed up his stuff, sprinted to the small reception area, and told their part-time receptionist to cancel whatever he had going on and that he would be gone for the day. Yessiree, money in the bank allowed him to make rash decisions like the one he'd just made. Not that he'd spent a penny of it. For some reason, he couldn't bring himself to touch his nest egg. As far as he knew, his mother hadn't spent any of it, either. He wondered about the why of it.

Alex hustled then, faster than he'd ever hustled in his life. He took all the back streets to reach the Symon brothers' office, where he picked up a thick white envelope, shook hands, and raced out of the building.

It took him forty extra minutes to reach the St. Cloud Oil offices, where he knew Jake would be coming in. It was beyond important that he be on-site when Jake set foot on dry land. There was no word that he could come up with to describe how important it was for Jake to know that he, Jake's brother, had done every single thing asked of him.

Jesus Christ, I have a brother! How wonderful is that?

While Alex waited for Jake, Jake was staring off into the distance as he waited for the boat that would take him home. He couldn't ever remember being so tired, so relieved. Another hour and he'd be back to his old life. He'd have to shower sixteen times to get the ripe, pungent smell off him. And then he'd have to go to the barber to get his head shaved before heading home to shower again and again. He knew it would take days, even weeks, before his pores expelled the stink of the oil. And it would take at least two weeks before he would be sporting hair on his head again. All he had to do was get the hell out of there, step into the boat, and not look back. Definitely not look back.

Jake saw the boat bearing down at the same moment he sensed a presence behind him. "You ready to say good-bye to this place, kid?"

"You know it, Zeke."

"Well, I'm the second one off, right behind you."

"Did you tell him?"

"Hell no! I like surprises. I can't wait to march my ass into human resources and claim my due." He laughed then, a rich cackle of merriment. Jake grinned when he saw four other oilmen line up behind Zeke.

"Looks like a full house. Ah, here *he* comes. I got your back, Zeke."

The speedboat roared to a stop. Jake reached for the rope ladder and tied it down. He knew he had to do or say something . . . Bullshit! He offered up a sloppy salute of sorts and swung himself over the side. He was going home. He could hear the raised voices of Zeke and the others, the lion roar of his father, then the cusswords that floated away on the strong wind. Then Zeke was standing next to him, grinning from ear to ear.

"That felt so damn good, kid. I shoulda done it a long time ago. Shoulda done a lot of things a long time ago."

"It's never too late, Zeke. That's what my mother used to tell me all the time. For a long time, I didn't get it, but when I did, I became a believer," Jake yelled, to be heard over the roar of the boat's engine.

"He's down five men now. He's probably feeling a little prickly. Don't you think?" Zeke guffawed. "He's gonna fight me with my pension and call this a mutiny, you wanna bet, kid?"

"Well, if he does, I know a hell of a lawyer . . ."

Sixty minutes later, the speedboat pulled to shore, and Jake and the others hit dry land. He saw the media first; and then he saw Alex. He waved to indicate that first he had to go through the gauntlet before he could make contact. Alex nodded to show he understood.

Jake tried to be brief, telling the reporters to talk to the men behind him; they did all the hard work. But the media weren't buying it. It took thirty minutes before he could shepherd Zeke and the others to the offices of St. Cloud Oil.

"Listen, Zeke, we all need a shower, clean clothes, and a few hours' sleep. Can you meet me at the Sizzler tonight? Around seven. I know you probably have plans, but it won't take long. It's important; otherwise, I wouldn't ask."

"Sure, kid, seven it is. You need a ride home?"

"Nah, I'm good. See ya." Jake walked away, toward where Alex was standing.

"Don't get too close—this stuff has a way of transferring itself to anything within reach. I'd shake your hand or hug you, but it just isn't wise."

Alex grinned. "Man, you could scare the hell out of anyone. You need a ride home?"

"Nah, I'm going to run home."

"Jake, it's ten miles, maybe a little more. C'mon, I have a blanket in the trunk."

"You'll never get the oil smell out of the car. Hey, I'm okay. Gotta get my land legs back, and I need to do some thinking. I think clearly when I'm running. Thanks for all you did for me. I appreciate it. I told Zeke I'd meet him at the Sizzler at seven. Can you make it?"

"Absolutely, I can make it. Guess I should hang on to this until tonight then, huh? Ya know, Jake, I couldn't find one damn *shack* anywhere on the beach."

Jake turned and roared, "*What?*"

"Oh, for God's sake, lighten up, Jake. While I couldn't find a shack, I did manage to find a twenty-one-hundred-square-foot beach house for nine hundred grand. You said money was no object, and the Symon brothers said it was a steal. My mother helped me get it ready. That means clean, new sheets and food—enough to last a few months. Booze stocked in the cabinets, fluffy yellow—I repeat, fluffy yellow—towels, firewood for cold nights. Every damn amenity you can think of. Zeke is good to go."

"And the wheels?"

"Brand-new Dodge Ram, all gassed up in the driveway. The only thing we couldn't come up with was a bevy of beautiful ladies for your friend. Mom said she didn't want any part of that, and he was on his own."

Jake started to laugh as he picked up his feet and started his ten-mile jog for home.

Alex stood there in the morning sun and watched his brother until he was out of sight. Then he turned and walked back to where he'd parked his car. He felt good. Damn good, in fact. So good, he was going to blow off the rest of the day, since he'd already told the receptionist to cancel any appointments he had. The only question was, what was he going to do with all that time? Well, if he thought about it long enough and hard enough, he was sure he'd come up with something. Still and all, it was a lot of hours to kill before it was time to meet up with Jake at the Sizzler.

Maybe he'd surprise his mother and head over to the bistro, where he could pitch in and help bus the tables or wait on customers; whatever his mother needed him to do. More than likely, she would just be glad to see him and would wait on him, serve him a delicious lunch, and if he was lucky, sit down with him for a few minutes. *Wise choice, Mr. Rosario,* he told himself as he turned over the engine.

Jake walked out of the barbershop, his bald head glistening in the midday sun. It was a beautiful day, no humidity at all, but it was, after all, the middle of October. Still, they had hot, muggy days in December and January. Regardless, he still smelled.

He was tired. The ten-mile run had about done him in, but the hot shower had helped for the three-mile run back to town. He needed wheels. He *definitely* needed a set of wheels, so he headed straight across town to the Landry car dealership, where he bought himself a new Dodge Ram and waited for them to spruce it up so he could drive it off the lot. He felt right at home behind the wheel—more so than he'd ever felt behind the wheel of the Porsche.

Jake drove home, discarded his clothes, and used the outside shower again to scrub down. He lathered up his bald head and scrubbed and scrubbed. He wrapped a towel around himself and entered the house, where he chowed down on a pizza he'd been smart enough to pick up a mile from home. He savored every last bite of it, crust and all. He washed it down with two bottles of beer from the fridge. *Now, maybe I can sleep*, he thought as he trudged up the stairs to his bedroom.

Jake dropped the towel and pulled on a pair of flannel shorts and one of his tattered LSU T-shirts. "Sleep, here I come," he muttered, just as the doorbell rang. He told himself he didn't have to go downstairs if he didn't want to. But maybe it was Alex, and something had gone awry. He groaned as he padded out of the room and downstairs. He opened the door, stunned to see his father standing in front of him.

"Can I come in, Jake? I need to talk to you."

"About what? Look, I helped you, I did what you wanted. I want you to leave me alone. No more favors. I hate you. You hate me, and yet here you are standing in my doorway after I saved your ass. Which, by the way, you never thanked me for. But, you know what? That's okay; just wait till you get my bill."

"Things," was the curt response to Jake's question. "A cup of coffee would go well about now. For some reason, coffee helps me over hurdles. With your mother, it was tea. She thought a cup of tea was the cure-all to everything in life."

Maybe it was the mention of his mother, maybe it was the strange look on his father's face, or maybe it was something totally unrelated to anything, but Jake opened the door wider and walked into the kitchen. He reached up for the can of coffee in the cabinet, sure that it was still good. He measured everything out, started the coffeemaker, and sat down at the table. "Should we wait for the coffee, or do you want to talk about those *things?*"

"Listen, Jake, first things first. Thanks. I know that doesn't mean much to you coming from me, but sometimes you need to say the words out loud. And you actually have to hear them. I know you hate me, and I'm sorry about that. To be honest, I hated you for a long time, but I don't hate you now, and I haven't for many, many years. I should have come here sooner or gone to wherever you were, but I didn't have the guts."

"You? No guts? What the hell are you talking about? We're done. There's nothing for either one of us to say, and whatever it is you *think* you need to say, I'm really not interested in hearing it."

"You may not *want* to hear it, but you *need* to hear it."

What Jake heard was the last plopping sound of the coffeemaker. He got up and poured two cups. Strong and black. He handed one over to his father, who wrapped both hands around the mug. He waited.

"This is about your mother, Jake."

"Oh, now, hold on there, Mr. St. Cloud. Let's not go there. I don't want to hear any crap that comes out of your mouth in regard to my mother."

Jonah ignored him as he stared out Jake's kitchen window. "I fell in love with your mother when we were both very young. She was the most beautiful creature I'd ever laid eyes on. I couldn't get over how much she loved me. Her family thought I wasn't good enough for her bloodline. She didn't care. We had this out-of-the-world wedding, and I can still remember every last little detail. There was nothing in the world I wouldn't have done for that woman. I tried to be one of those blue bloods, but it just wasn't in me, and it was your mother who said I should just be who I was. And it worked. We never said a cross word to one another. She was my life, Jake.

"Then you came along. God, I remember that day as though it were yesterday. I went out and bought a red wagon, a pitcher's mitt, a tricycle, and all kinds of stuff for you, and you were just a few hours old. Your mother laughed and laughed. It was without a doubt the happiest day of my life.

"And life was good, wonderful, beautiful, and I could not have asked for more. I didn't want more, and if there was more to be had, I didn't want to hear about it."

Jake watched his father, saw the torment in his eyes, and started to feel sick to his stomach.

"On your third birthday, we had a party for you. You were so rambunctious back then. You liked the paper and the boxes better than the gifts. Your mother and I laughed about that. After all the guests went home, and you were put to bed, your mother took me into the parlor and said she needed to talk to me about something. I was happy to go, and whatever it was she wanted to talk to me about, I was sure it was going to be something wonderful.

"But it wasn't wonderful at all." Jake watched as his father licked at his dry lips, took a swallow of coffee, and continued. "What your mother told me was that two days before our wedding, an old beau of hers came to visit one evening. She had asked him to visit because, as she said to me, she wanted to make sure she didn't have any lingering feelings for the old beau. Well, there must have been lingering feelings. The old beau took the love of my life to bed and impregnated her. My happy, wonderful, beautiful world ended right there, that very moment in time. Your mother told me she just couldn't keep living with the lie of your paternity on her conscience.

"When I asked her who the man was, she refused to tell me. I got up, left the house, and went on a drunken binge. I didn't go back for weeks, and when I did, it was as though nothing had happened. Your mother moved into her own bedroom, and that was the end of our marriage. I guess you can figure out the rest. I wanted to tell you many times, but I couldn't. I thought it was your mother's place to tell you. She's the one who insisted on the lie.

"When your mother was in the hospital, I thought for sure she would tell you and not go to her grave with that awful cross she was carrying. That's why I stayed away. And no, I was not with another woman. Actually, I was lurking in the hospital like some depraved creature. I would walk by her room when I knew no one was around. I wore a silly disguise that was so stupid I can't even believe I did it."

Jake felt as if he'd been kicked in the gut not once but repeatedly. He couldn't get his tongue to work. All he could do was stare at his father, or rather the man he thought of as his father.

"I see you're in shock, Jake. I'm sorry. You know, I feel like a load of bricks was just taken off my shoulders."

Jake finally found his tongue. "And dumped them on my shoulders."

"Yeah. Listen, I don't know if it was right or wrong of me to tell you. I didn't tell you to tarnish your memory of your mother. God, Jake, there are no words to tell you how much I loved that woman. I couldn't get past the betrayal. I tried, but nothing I did worked."

"Who . . . what's my father's name?"

"Ah yes, what's that term you like to use so much? Sperm donor? Are you sure you want to know?"

Jake didn't know if he did or not, but he nodded.

"Clement Trousoux. Retired United States senator. He lives in the Garden District in New Orleans. I guess I might as well tell you about him and what I did. At first, your mother wouldn't tell me his name, but I finally got it out of her when she was in the hospital that last time.

"I went to Washington about six months after she died, found him, and got in his face, as young people say today. Guess what he said to me? He said it didn't mean anything, it was just a roll in the hay. I beat the goddamn living hell out of him. I left him so bloodied and broken, I thought for sure I would be arrested. I think I broke every bone in his body. The news reports said he was mugged and robbed. He was in the hospital for months. Go figure that one."

Jake didn't know if he could figure that one or not. He was simply too shocked and too speechless. When he could speak again, all he said was, "I remember reading something about

Senator Trousoux's being attacked when I was in my freshman year at LSU. That was your doing, huh?"

Jonah stood up. "Yeah, it was. I guess I don't have anything else to say. I know I rocked your world, Jake, but I got to thinking. Sooner or later, you're going to be getting married, and you'll need to know about health issues if you plan on having a family. And for whatever it's worth, I'm sorry as hell you aren't my son. I mean that. You're a good man, Jake. If you ever need a job, one will be waiting for you."

"My name . . ."

"You're stuck with it unless you want to change it, and that's going to open up all kinds of cans of worms. I'd be proud for you to carry on the St. Cloud name, but it's up to you. Do we shake hands here, smile at each other? I don't know how we should end this."

Jake didn't know, either. "How about we just say good-bye, and I thank you for stopping by."

"That'll work. At least for now."

Jake walked Jonah St. Cloud to the door.

"I care about only one thing. I want you to understand that I so loved your mother, there are just no words to tell you how much. She was everything to me. That's why I never could commit to getting a divorce and moving on. I was stuck in that time warp. Your mother understood and forgave me. That's what *you* carry away from this, Jake."

Jake didn't think he'd ever heard anything

so final in his life as when the door closed behind his father. He leaned up against it, closed his burning eyes, then slid to the floor, where he cried like a baby.

It's never too late.

Chapter 10

Jake rolled over and groaned. Something was wrong with his neck; it hurt like hell. It took several moments to realize he was on the floor. It all came back to him in one wild *swoosh. Son of a bitch!* He blinked to ward off a wave of dizziness. He cursed again, long and loud, before he struggled to his feet. He tried to massage his neck but all that did was create more pain. He trudged to the kitchen, where he eyed the cold coffee in the pot. He looked at the two empty cups on the table. He picked up the one his father—oops, that man who was not his father after all—had used, and pitched it with such force against the refrigerator that it shattered into a thousand minuscule pieces.

Jake forced himself to rinse the pot and

scoop fresh grounds into the wire basket. What he probably needed then was a quart bottle of whiskey to drown his sorrows instead of a cup of Cajun coffee. It wasn't like either one was going to solve a thing. Tea. Maybe he should make hot tea. Scratch that; he wasn't a tea drinker, never had been. He sat down at the table and dropped his head into his hands. *Now what the hell am I supposed to do? What is the politically correct thing to do now that I've been robbed of a no-account father and a brother I've dreamed of finding for the last eighteen years?*

His thoughts took him back in time to that day in the hospital when his mother was dying. She'd said at some point he was going to hear things and not to think too harshly of her. She'd made him promise. How many promises had he made that day? Three? Four? Did it even matter? He needed to talk to someone. Who? Alex? If he talked to Alex, he'd have to tell him the truth, that he wasn't his brother. Did he really want to do that? Couldn't he pretend a little while longer that he had a brother? What would be so wrong about doing that?

A lie is a lie is a lie, his conscience pricked. *So, okay,* he responded to his conscience, *I'll tell him, but where is it written that I have to do it today or even tomorrow?* His conscience demanded to know why the procrastination, and he responded in kind. *Just because I want to keep the feeling of belonging to someone. What's so wrong about that?*

A lie is a lie is a lie.

Talk about a rock and a hard place. Jake's thoughts took him to all kinds of weird places as he sipped at the hot, strong coffee. He was officially alone in the big wide world. There were no buffers between him and his mortality. No siblings. No aunts or uncles, no cousins. No nothing. The only way he could ever have a family now was if he found some woman dumb enough to marry him. He wondered what the chances of *that* ever happening were? He wanted to cry. Maybe he should cry.

Big boys don't cry. Who said that? Jonah St. Cloud, that's who. Well, screw you, Jonah St. Cloud. I'll bawl my eyes out if I feel like it and there's not a damn thing you can do about it.

Jake finished his cup of coffee, all the while eyeing the shattered cup on the floor. Sooner or later, he was going to have to clean that up. *Yeah, later. A whole lot later.* He got up, stepped around the shards on the floor, and poured himself another cup of coffee. He sat down to finish thinking.

Whoa! Whoa! Whoa! He realized that he did have a buffer. Of sorts. He really did have a sperm donor out there. In the blink of an eye, Jake was off his chair and galloping up the stairs to the second floor. He grabbed his laptop and ran back down to the kitchen. "Let's just see who you really are, you piece-of-shit person," Jake muttered as he hit the Google button and typed in the name Clement Trousoux.

Whoa! again as article after article appeared on the screen. And a rogues' gallery of pictures. Well, son of a bitch, he did look a little like the sperm donor staring at him from the computer.

Jake had always prided himself on his exceptional memory. He read and read until his eyes started to ache. He sat back for a while as he sifted and collated all that he'd read. He filed the articles in his mind for easy reference. When he was finished, he went to the gallery of pictures and paid close attention to what he was seeing. The man looked very virile, strong, capable, assured; the kind of look that lots of money in the bank seemed to give certain people. That particular look completely vanished around . . . Jake's mind whirled as he calculated the date. Jake's freshman year at LSU, six months after his mother died, Clement Trousoux's life changed. He'd been mugged; his recuperation was long and painful. His face had been reconstructed. He limped. He used a cane. He had no feeling in his left arm at all; nerve damage. But according to the caption, Clement had soldiered on to serve his magnificent birth state of Louisiana.

Four weddings. Two deaths and one divorce. Two wealthy women who left their estates to Clement on their deathbeds. Wife number three, the divorcée, had swooped in and snatched all that away and was now a well-known belly dancer in the French Quarter, with boy toys at her beck and call. When some nosy person had the gall to ask her about Clement Trousoux, she always responded with *Clement who?*

Jake continued to peruse the wall of pictures. Clement with a tennis racquet, Clement on the links holding up a four iron. Clement standing by a small private plane that he owned, Clement in scuba diving gear. Jake wanted to gag as he continued to peruse the wall of pictures. Ah, there's the fourth marriage. A close-up of the new bride. Three thoughts raced through Jake's mind. *Trophy wife. Trashy gold digger. Breast implants.* Clement looked like a doddering old fool posing with his cane in a cutaway suit. He was smiling, but it looked more like a grimace to Jake.

It was all crap with a big red bow. Jake bolted from the kitchen and ran into his family room. He needed sound—music. Within minutes, the jazz he loved could be heard throughout the house. Miles Davis. Coltrane. Lou Donaldson.

Jazz was Jake's passion, as it had been his mother's. With the first perfect notes of "Light Foot" from Donaldson's sax, Jake felt all the tension and stress seep out of his body.

As Jake continued to read everything there was to read about Clement Trousoux, Donaldson gave way to Miles Davis's *Kind of Blue*, the best-selling jazz album of all time.

Jake wished he could just shut out everything, go into his jazz trance, and listen forever and ever. But it was not to be. Jazz was where he went when he needed to escape; jazz was where he went when the world invaded his being. His own private oasis where no one could get to him.

Time lost all meaning for Jake as he worked the computer and listened to his beloved jazz. Suddenly he was aware of the silence in the house. He looked up at the clock over the doorway and realized that he had less than thirty minutes to get dressed and head for the Sizzler. He moved his feet and was out of the house and behind the wheel of his new Dodge Ram and on his way in record time. He arrived just as Alex pulled into the parking lot from the opposite direction.

God Almighty, how am I going to tell Alex he's not my brother? How am I going to tell him all the rest of the crap, too? Very, very carefully was the best he could come up with. Now, though, he had to put on his game face and get Zeke settled. He waited, his stomach in knots, for Alex to cross the parking lot, a huge grin on his face as he waved the white envelope in the air.

They both saw Zeke at the same moment as he and his ancient forty-year-old truck, more rust than metal, belching smoke, came to a shuddering stop in the middle of the parking lot.

"I think that hunk of junk just coughed out its last snort. Methinks, bro, you got Zeke that new set of wheels just in time. So, what's the game plan here? Do we eat first, or do we take him to his new digs and come back here?"

Alex called me bro. Jake's stomach did a somersault. "I say we take him out there first. You can drive."

"Works for me."

Jake introduced Alex to Zeke. The men all shook hands. Jake eyed Zeke's clean-shaven face and bald head.

"Lookin' good, Zeke. Change of plans. We need to go somewhere first. It's still early. What do you say?"

"Makes me no never mind," Zeke said, crawling into the backseat of Alex's Mustang. "Now that I am officially retired, time has no meaning." He cackled.

"Where are we going, if you don't mind me asking? Please tell me it isn't to a confrontation with your old man."

"It's not. I want to show you something and ask your opinion. Won't take long, Zeke."

The men made small talk as Alex expertly maneuvered in and out of traffic till he got to a scrubby-looking turnoff. He turned right and plowed forward, finally coming to a full stop at a gate that was standing open. Palm trees and lush palmettos were everywhere. To Jake, it looked like a mini paradise.

"Everyone out!" Alex bellowed.

"What is this place, Jake?" Zeke asked, looking around.

Alex handed the thick white envelope over to Jake, who, in turn, handed it to Zeke. "This place is *yours*, Zeke. All bought and paid for. No one can ever take it away from you. And those wheels, they're yours, too. You are officially retired in style, Zeke. The only thing missing is that string of ladies you hold such store by. I'd like to make a suggestion. Get a dog!"

"Mine! This is mine? Jake, I know you mean well, but I can't afford this place. Not on my retirement."

"Did you miss that part about it's all bought and paid for? And the taxes and insurance come out of a trust fund that goes with the house. The truck, too. Listen, Zeke, this is a drop in the bucket in the way of repayment for all you've done for me when . . . well, you know when. You'll really hurt my feelings if you don't accept it. This is all the paperwork. Keep it someplace safe. Shall we take the tour?"

Zeke wiped his eyes on the sleeve of his wrinkled but clean shirt as he followed Jake and Alex into the house for the tour.

Fifteen minutes later, Zeke, his eyes red and wet, gave both young men bone-crushing hugs. Then he stood back and shrugged. "Whatever the words are, I don't have them, boys. Thanks. Listen, do you mind if I don't go back to the Sizzler with you? I'd kind of like to sit here on this fine porch and look at the posies in those crocks and maybe have a beer or two."

"No problem. You okay with us getting rid of that bucket of bolts you left back at the Sizzler?"

"Damn straight. I'm not dreaming, am I, son?"

There was that word. "No, Zeke, it's for real. There is one thing, though. You might like to take a spin in your new truck tomorrow and go by Rosario's Bistro and thank Alex's mother for providing your food supply and decorating your house. You better make sure you water all those plants she got you, and don't be taking those yellow towels to the beach, either. There might be some other dos and don'ts, so check with her. Her name, by the way, is Sophia. You have a standing two-week food delivery and a booze delivery, but go easy on that last, Zeke, so you can enjoy all this. Remember, get yourself a dog for company."

"I'll do that, son. I purely will." Zeke held out his hand. His grip was like forged iron.

"You know where I live, Zeke. You need anything, come on by. We can listen to some Miles Davis, a little Coltrane, and pound a few."

A tear rolled down Zeke's cheek. "I'll do that, son. Can I bring my dog?"

That word again. Jake laughed as he waved good-bye.

Alex turned the key in the engine. "Damn, I feel good, and I didn't even do anything. You feeling good, Jake? I didn't know you were into jazz."

"Zeke gave my . . . Jonah St. Cloud a hun-

151

dred percent. I bet you'll be surprised to know Zeke is only fifty-eight. He looks seventy-eight, but he isn't. That's what life on the rigs does to you. He's a good, kind, gentle man. That's why all the ladies go after him. He'd have you believe he's a skirt chaser and a real boozer, but he isn't. He's just a hell of a great guy, and I feel damn lucky to have worked with him. He taught me everything I know and then some."

"Sounds a little to me like Zeke is lucky to have you in his life. Do you think he'll get a dog?"

"Oh yeah, he might even beat me to it. That's on the top of my own to-do list. I hope I can get one tomorrow."

"Good for you. Man, I am so hungry I could eat a wooden chair."

"I need to talk to you about something, Alex."

"Ohhh, that sounds serious." Alex took his eyes off the road for a moment. "Something tells me I'm not going to like whatever it is."

"I don't know. Maybe you will. I don't want to ruin our dinner, so let's wait for the discussion until we're finished. Just for the record, I plan on getting falling-down drunk, so don't let me drive."

"Well, if you're going to get falling-down drunk, then so am I. I'll call my mother to put her on alert that she might have to drive us home. From the day I got my driving permit, she made me promise to call her no matter where I was or what time it was if I was drinking, so she could come pick me up. You okay with that? Doesn't mean I'm a mama's boy," Alex said defensively.

"That's a good thing, Alex. Don't apologize. It's good to have someone care enough about you to do things like that."

"Now that that's out of the way, tell me about your interests in jazz. I've had a secret desire all my life to be a country-western singer. Willie Nelson and Clint Black are my idols. I just love country music. The thing is, I can't carry a note. Mom said I sound like a cat in distress. I think she called it caterwauling, or something like that."

"No kidding. I never would have pegged you for country music. You play any instruments?"

"Guitar. Self-taught. I'll leave it to you to figure out how good I am at it. How about you?"

"Piano. I had years of lessons. Forced lessons. I don't even own a piano."

"Well, we're here. I want the biggest steak on the menu, with a load of those thick potato wedges that come with horseradish sauce, and the grilled asparagus. And you can pick up the tab, bro. Hey, how's it feel being bald?"

Jake slid out of the car. "I feel naked. Takes two weeks for it to sprout back. You gotta shave it off, or the smell stays with you. Once you come off a rig, everyone heads for the nearest barber. You saw Zeke. The man has the thickest head of hair of anyone I've ever seen. And he always prided himself on that beard of his. He'll let it grow in again. He says it defines who he is. A man with a lot of hair and a beard." Jake guffawed.

Inside, Jake asked for a booth in the back.

"Pretty damn dark in here," Alex said as he motioned to the dark paneling and the deep burgundy leather booths.

"Yeah, it is kind of dark; it's even darker in the back, but what the hell. There's enough light to see to eat and drink. That's what we're here for, right?"

"And for you to tell me whatever it is you think I might not like to hear," Alex said, following the hostess to the last booth in the room.

"That, too. Right now our first big decision is do we drink beer by the bottle or by the pitcher? By the pitcher means one for you and one for me. They automatically keep bringing new ones, unlike when you order by the bottle—sometimes you have to wait for them."

"Then by all means let's go by the pitcher. What's our limit?"

"There is *no* limit, Alex."

"That serious, huh?" At the expression on Jake's face, he mumbled, "Oh shit!"

Oh shit was right.

The beer came.

The food came.

More beer came.

And still more beer came.

When the waitress cleared away their plates, she asked if they had a ride home.

"We do, young lady," Alex said, his eyes crossing for her enjoyment. "Do you want us to pay our bill now?"

"That would be nice as I'm going off duty in another twenty minutes, and I'd like to close out my drawer."

"My brother is paying tonight, aren't you, bro?"

"I am paying." Jake squinted down at the tab, added a very generous tip, and closed out his bill. Then he started a new one with a new waitress. "See how easy that was?"

"Yeah, that was easy. So, let's talk, Jake, before I'm too drunk to understand what you're going to tell me."

Jake talked and Alex listened, for almost an hour and two more pitchers of beer, before Jake would allow Alex to ask questions.

Alex knuckled his eyes. "Okay. The only thing that bothers me is that you aren't my brother. I was just getting used to you. Ah shit, you dumb jerk, you sneaked your way into my heart when I wasn't looking. I just told you my big secret, a secret no one else in the world knows except my mother—that I aspire to be a country-western singer. You don't tell shit like that to anyone but your mother or your brother."

Jake was all choked up. "I won't tell anyone, Alex. Your secret is safe with me."

"See! See! That's what a real brother would say, then later on, when he gets pissed off at you for whatever reason, he threatens to tell but would never really do it. I don't care what they say, I want you for my brother. We don't have to tell anyone, Jake."

"No more lies, Alex. My whole life was a lie. Think about that!"

"I don't want to think about that, Jake. Let's go to that guy's house, the one who spawned you, and beat the shit out of him for a second time. I'm a lawyer, I'll get us out of it. Hey, did you see on the news that Judge Spindler is retiring this weekend? There's going to be a big party."

"Big whoopee! Who cares? Certainly not me. You want his job, Alex?"

Alex drained his glass of beer and started to laugh. "A Latino judge! Oh yeah."

"After we kill that son of a bitch who had his way with my mother, we can work on that," Jake said drunkenly.

Alex leaned forward. "When are we going to do the dirty, bro?"

"How about tomorrow after we sober up?"

"Okay," Alex said agreeably. "Your mother wouldn't want you to do that, would she?"

"No. She should have told me, Alex. I have no one. You can't count that . . . that . . . that person who spawned me, and once we kill him, there is no one. This is too sad."

"You have me, Jake. And my mother. She doesn't even know you, but she loves you anyway because she knows I love you. And you have Zeke. I think that Fancy person might grow to love you, too."

"Yeah, and pigs fly." Jake picked up his empty pitcher and waved it around. It was refilled within seconds.

"How do you feel, Jake, about you-know-who not being your father?"

Jake was drunk enough to let it all come out. "Jealous at first that you had a father, such as he is, and I didn't have one. Betrayed by my mother and how she betrayed him. I did believe him when he said how much he loved her, but I guess he didn't love her enough to forgive her. Isn't love all about forgiveness, Alex?"

"You're asking the wrong person, bro. My mother told me women are funny creatures, and men will never, ever understand them. I think she's right," Alex said fretfully. "That means women are superior to us men. That makes me itch."

"So scratch," Jake said, then burst out laughing. "Hey, you want to come home with me? We can have a sleepover. I can play my jazz favorites for you, and you can sing me some country-western ditties. That way we can get an early start to . . . you know, killing that skunk who spawned me."

"That makes sense. I have to call my mother if I can find my phone."

"Oops! Don't look now, Alex, but I think she's standing in the doorway, and, holy shit, Zeke is with her. That is Zeke, isn't it?"

Alex squinted. "Yep, that's Zeke, all right. And he's with my mother. This is not good, Jake. Two of them against the two of us, and one of them is a woman, my very own mother. Mum's the word, okay?"

The dark-haired woman, Zeke at her side, approached the table. "Hello, boys. I understand you need a ride home. Follow me—your chariot awaits. Meet my new best friend, Zeke Anders. He came by the bistro to thank me for what I did for him. He was worried about you two, and now I can see why."

Jake tried his best to straighten up. "It's all my fault. I coerced Alex. He didn't want to get drunk—I insisted. Hi there, Zeke. I thought we tucked you in for the night. Tell this nice lady what a rascal I am and not to blame her son."

"It's all a lie, Mom. I came of my own free will, and I drank way more than Jake did. I was just going to call you for a ride home. Home to Jake's house—we're having a sleepover because we are going to . . ."

"Have a bad hangover in the morning," Jake said quickly. He pretended not to see the strange look on Zeke's face. *Dammit, nothing is going right tonight.*

"How do you want to handle this, Zeke?" Sophia Rosario asked sweetly. "I'm sure you have more experience at things like this than I do."

"How about this, Miss Sophia? I'll drive them to Jake's in Alex's car and come back in the morning for my new truck. I think I can handle it. See if these two galoots owe any more money on the bill."

Alex reared up and almost fell over for his efforts. "You sweet-talking my mother, Zeke?"

"Uh-huh. She invited me for dinner tomorrow. You got anything to say about that, son?"

Alex opted for the high road. "Nope."

"That's what I thought. C'mon now, let's get you two drunks out to the car. I thought you could hold your liquor, boy," Zeke hissed in Jake's ear.

"Yeah, well, tonight was a little out of the ordinary, Zeke. I'll tell you all about it sometime."

Zeke nodded, his bald head gleaming under the bright fluorescent light in the foyer of the restaurant.

Outside in the crisp night air, Jake snapped to attention. He knew he was drunker than he'd ever been in his whole life, and he'd been on some serious drunks in his thirty-five years. He wasn't sure, but he thought this was Alex's first serious drunk. He'd corrupted poor Alex. Well, he'd have to make that right tomorrow. Tomorrow, he'd kill Clement Trousoux all by himself. He'd sneak out before Alex woke up and do the dirty deed and be back at the house in time to make him breakfast, and no one would be the wiser.

Boy, was he ever drunk.

Chapter 11

Zeke Anders looked at the digital clock on Jake's stove. The second the clock turned over to the number six, he was on his feet and barreling up the stairs, where, like some angry drill sergeant, he shouted at the top of his lungs, "Up and at 'em, boys!"

"What the hell!" Jake bellowed. He cracked one eye. "Zeke, what the hell are you doing here? What time is it?"

A voice, cursing ripely, came from down the hall. "Is there a fire? Did the alarm go off?"

"It's six o'clock, and I've been out to the store already, so get your lazy asses in the shower so I can go home to my new digs. I'm too old to be babysitting the likes of you two. And I don't give a good rat's ass if you two have the queen mother of all hangovers or not. You

161

play, you pay. How many times did I tell you that, Jake?"

"A thousand. Okay, two thousand," Jake grumbled as he swung his legs over the side of the bed. He felt like his head was going to spin right off his neck. "Why are you here, anyway?"

"Because that pretty lady at the Eye-talian restaurant asked me to bring you two home. Sweetest lady I ever met. How could I say no? She invited me to lunch. I think she recognized my sterling qualities."

Jake wanted to laugh when he heard Alex yelling for Zeke to stay away from his mother, but his head hurt too bad.

Thirty minutes later, Jake and Alex trooped into the kitchen. Both looked at Zeke with a jaundiced eye, then they spied the aspirin bottle and the two tall glasses of tomato juice that both knew Zeke had doctored up.

"Now I got things to do and places to go, so tell me right now what the hell got into the two of you last night. And don't even think about lying to me."

Jake looked at Alex.

Alex looked at Jake.

Alex shrugged, and Jake licked at his lips.

"Okay, let's hear it!"

Jake was like a runaway train as he repeated everything just the way he'd told it to Alex the night before. Then he took a deep breath and swallowed the tomato juice in one long gulp. Alex did the same.

"And your game plan is . . ."

"When our heads clear up, we're going to New Orleans, to the Garden District, so I can kill Clement Trousoux. Alex is my lawyer; he's going to make sure I don't go to jail. Then I'm going to get a dog. After that, I'm coming back here to chill out," Jake said, a wild look in his eyes.

"It sounded like a good plan last night," Alex mumbled.

Jake looked at the dozen or so jelly dough-nuts sitting on the table. He plucked one off the plate and jammed it into his mouth. "It's still a good plan," he blustered. "Why aren't you saying anything, Zeke?"

"Because I'm speechless, that's why. I knew you boys were drunk, but I didn't think you were *that* drunk. There's nothing worse than a stupid drunk. Especially one I helped raise. Dumb shits. Both of you are dumb shits," Zeke repeated, to make sure the two of them got it.

Jake had the grace to look ashamed. As did Alex.

"Dammit, Zeke, don't you even care about all that other stuff I just told you about? My mother, Jonah, how they both lied to me all my life? I don't have anyone now. I wanted a brother all my life, and I thought I had one. Now, I'm this . . . this *orphan!*"

"Oh, boohoo," Zeke said. "You're all growed up, son. So you got dealt a body blow unlike anything you ever experienced. You deal with it and move on. Your mother was human, just like the rest of us. I'd say she did one fine job of raising you. That's what counts in the end. Right now, though, I'm thinking she wouldn't be all that proud of you. As for Jonah, let me play devil's advocate here. Can't say I wouldn't have done the same thing. You see, Jake, you just never know how it's going to play out until you're standing in that pair of shoes, because Jonah is human, too. I'm sure he has regrets. You even said he did. Think about this. Jonah got his revenge, but what good did it do him? He was still estranged from your mother, his wife. His life was . . . hell, you know what his life has been like. I don't think the man has had a happy day in his whole entire life since all that went down. You need to think about that, too. So Jonah broke just about every bone in that skunk's body for having his way with your mother. Who did that help? *No one* is the answer, except that Clement what's-his-name was crippled for life. He didn't even know about you until Jonah told him. Had he known, he might have done something, come forward, tried to make it right. I'm thinking if someone damn near killed me, I'd stay as far away from that person as I could get. What I'm saying here, Jake, is you just don't know, and because you don't know, you can't go off half-cocked and do something that's going to ruin the rest of your life."

Alex was still in his mumbling mood. He reached for one of the sugary doughnuts. "He has a point, Jake." At least that's what Jake thought he said.

"Finish up, boys. Then we can go back to the Sizzler to pick up your vehicle, Jake. And if you still want to go to see *that man,* I'll drive you. But only if you can contain yourselves and commit no violence. I don't have a problem with your confronting him. I also don't have a problem with your asking him what he has to say. So, what's it going to be?"

Jake looked across the table at Alex, who shrugged, meaning *whatever you want to do is okay with me.*

"Okay, let's hit it, then," Jake said, getting up from the table. "By the way, Zeke, thanks for bringing us home last night."

"Yeah, thanks. How pissed was my mother?" Alex asked.

"That's between you and her, son. C'mon now, time is money, as Ben Franklin said. Didn't rightly know that he was in the oil business."

Jake and Alex followed Zeke out of the house like two errant puppies following their big, strong leader, and got into Alex's car.

Forty-five minutes later, Zeke pulled into a gas station. "Just out of curiosity, do either one of you two geniuses have the address to where we're going? I can't be sure of this, but I don't think the man is in the phone book."

"We can ask when we get to the Garden District," Jake said. "Someone is sure to know where he lives."

Alex whipped out his cell phone. "Hold on— keep driving, Zeke. I know how we can get it." He called his office and issued orders like he knew what he was doing. Ten minutes later, his cell phone rang. He listened and said, "Got it. Thanks, Nick."

"You actually got it?" Zeke said, sounding impressed.

"Pays to have friends in the tax office. Everyone has to pay taxes on their property." He handed the phone to Jake and told him to type the address into the GPS.

No more than fifteen minutes had gone by when Jake heard the robotic voice on the GPS instruct Zeke to make a turn off St. Charles Avenue onto Prytania Street. Zeke followed the instructions and pulled to the curb. All three men got out and gawked at the beautiful mansion set back from a lush lawn and exquisite shrubbery and early-autumn flowers.

"This guy needs a shuttle service from here to the front door," Zeke observed. "I know who this family is—they're in banking, and they were big in the slave trade back in the day. I read up on this at one time. I even took the tour with a lady I was seeing at the time. The lady was more into architecture than she was into me. Come along, boys. Let's get this show on the road. You rehearsing what you're going to say, son?"

"I'm going to play it by ear, Zeke. Relax, I am not going to kill the son of a bitch."

"If you change your mind, I know I can get you off," Alex said as he rubbed his temples. "Damn, this is the worst headache I've ever had."

"Serves you right," Zeke snapped, showing the young lawyer no mercy.

Zeke was the only one huffing and puffing when Jake banged a monster lion's-head door knocker. Even he stepped back when he heard the overly loud sound inside the house.

The door was opened by a little maid in a gray uniform and white apron with a little hat of some kind on top of her curly hair.

Alex stepped forward. "Alexander Rosario, attorney-at-law, to see Mr. Clement Trousoux."

"Is Mr. Trousoux expecting you? He didn't say anything about early-morning visitors."

"Actually, no. Judge Spindler sent me. I mean us. We don't have a lot of time, so if you'd just direct us to where we can speak with the senator, I would appreciate it. I'm due back in court."

"Oh my, that does sound serious. Follow me. The senator is taking his morning coffee in the solarium."

Alex grinned and winked at Jake, who scowled at him.

Jake didn't know what he had expected, but the shriveled, wizened man sitting in a huge chair wasn't it. A walker, a cane, and a wheelchair stood nearby. A television set was on, but the man himself was staring off into space with a coffee mug clasped in both hands.

"Mr. Trousoux, these gentlemen are here from the court. Shall I bring fresh coffee, sir?"

Clement Trousoux looked up at his guests. Jake saw the milky white cataract on his right

167

eye. He stared long and hard and was relieved to see that he didn't bear much resemblance to the man in the big chair. At least he didn't think so. Thank God he took after his mother's side of the family.

Zeke waved the maid off, declining the coffee, then shut the door behind her. He thought twice before he snapped the lock.

Trousoux looked up at the three imposing-looking men. "Isn't it a little early in the morning to come calling?"

"Alex Rosario, attorney-at-law," Alex said. "These two gentlemen are my . . . associates. Zeke Anders and Jake St. Cloud."

Jake saw the crippled body stiffen in the big chair. "Well now, that's a name I recognize. You here to finish the job for Jonah?"

"I'd like to, but no, that's not why we're here," Jake said through clenched teeth.

"Then why are you here? I was having a nice day till you showed up," the old man said coldly.

"I just want some answers. Give them to me, and we'll leave," Jake said, trying to control the rage he was feeling.

"In order to get answers, you have to ask the questions. Go ahead and ask. Doesn't mean I'll answer them. I do have a question of my own first, though. Did Jonah send you here?"

"No. I came on my own, with Alex and Zeke. I didn't find out . . . about you until yesterday. I would have come sooner had I known."

There was silence from the big chair. A bony

hand reached over to the remote, and the soft voices on the television morning show were reduced to silence.

"Why? I guess that's the question of the day," Jake said.

To his credit, the man in the big chair made no pretense of not understanding what he was being asked. "It was a long time ago. Selma was my first love, and I did love her. When she told me she was breaking off our relationship because she had met this . . . man who, she said, made her blood sing, I was devastated. The man was Jonah St. Cloud. I couldn't believe it at first because there was no bloodline there that was . . . acceptable to me. In the end, I had to accept it because that's what a man does under such circumstances. A year went by, and I heard through friends that Selma was engaged to be married. I almost killed myself when I heard that. I thought, hoped, she'd come to her senses and want me back. It didn't happen."

"What did happen?" Alex asked before Jake could get the words out of his own mouth.

"A week or so before the wedding, Selma called me and asked me to come by. I was so sure there was going to be a reconciliation. I didn't sleep for days. I was worse than any woman choosing what to wear—I got a haircut, the whole nine yards. My father, a very wise old man, tried to talk to me, as did my friends. They didn't want me to get my hopes up, then crash if the meeting turned out to be something other than what I was hoping for. Needless to say, I didn't listen."

For one crazy moment, as Jake looked at the man sitting in the big chair, he knew somehow that the senator was dying. He wished he'd stayed home. Suddenly he didn't want to hear what his father was going to say.

"Anyway, Selma greeted me cordially. We talked about silly things, she asked how I was, banal conversation. All I wanted to do was take her in my arms, pledge my undying love, and kiss her until we both passed out. She said she appreciated my coming over and that she just wanted to see me to make sure she wasn't making a mistake in marrying Jonah. I don't think she had any idea what those words did to me. I knew by the look on her face, the joy in her eyes, that Jonah, not me, was the one and only one for her. I went crazy. I forced myself on her. Whether you believe me or not, I have no clear recollection of what happened after that. What I do remember clearly, however, was how hard she was crying and her saying when I left that she would never, ever forgive me. So, yes, I am guilty of . . ."

"Raping my mother?" Jake said through clenched teeth.

"At the time I didn't see it that way, but yes, that would be the truth. I went back to school and went on a binge drinking spree. I lived in fear that Selma would tell Jonah, and he would come and kill me. Actually, I wanted to kill myself, but that's neither here nor there. The wedding went off as scheduled. The happy couple went off on a honeymoon and returned to set up housekeeping, as they say. Life went on. For them. Not for me."

"Until?" Zeke said.

"After your third birthday, Selma told Jonah that he was not your father. Then she told me about you. But she warned me that if Jonah ever found out who I was, he might kill me, so I should please, please, stay away and not try to see you. For years, I lived in fear of what Jonah would do.

"And then, years later, about six months after Selma died, Jonah paid me a visit in Washington. It was the year I became chairman of the Senate Judiciary Committee. I was at home, putting some books on a shelf, when he walked in. No one was there but me, and when I saw him lock the door, I knew what was coming. I wanted to die. I really did.

"Jonah pulled out a picture of you. It was a Polaroid shot of you opening your birthday presents. He threw it at me and said how he wanted me to see you the day he learned that you were not his son, the day he lost everything he cared about in his life.

"I was so intent on what he was saying, looking at the picture of you at the age of three, that I didn't care about anything else. He damn near beat me to death, and I didn't defend myself. What I did was cry like some sniveling little pantywaist. I took the beating because I deserved it. All I asked was that, at some point, I would get to meet you. Before I blacked out for the last time, Jonah bent down and said that if I ever tried to see you, get in touch with you, he would . . . he would . . ."

The three men stared at Trousoux as each of them tried to imagine the beating the man had undergone.

"What did he threaten you with?" Jake asked.

"He said he would . . . kill you. Mother of God, I believed him. That's why I never tried . . ."

Jake drew a deep breath. He moved then and placed his hands on the arms of the big chair. He leaned so close, his nose almost touched Trousoux's. "The question at the moment is, did you *want* to get in touch with me?"

"What kind of stupid question is that, young man? Of course I did. I went to as many of your high-school football games as I could, and every one of your college football games your freshman year at LSU. But I couldn't take the risk that Jonah meant what he said.

"I will go to my grave loving your mother. How could I risk his killing her son—my son?

"Do you see that big, battered steamer trunk in the corner? It belonged to my grandfather. That's what I'm leaving you in my will; that and nothing more. In case you haven't figured it out yet, I'm dying. I'm on borrowed time right now. According to my doctors, I should have been pushing up daisies this past Easter. I'm still here but not for long. I'm tired now. If there's nothing else, I'd like to be left in peace.

"Oh, there is one more thing. When your

mother was in the hospital, I went to see her. More than once, actually. She said she forgave me. We had long, comfortable conversations. She had mixed feelings about the situation, but she was heavily medicated. She told me that Jonah knew that he was not your father but that she had never told him who was. One minute she wanted you to know the truth, then the next minute, she didn't. She made me promise not to tell you until after she was gone. And she said it would be all right with her if I took the secret to my grave. She was so guilt-ridden.

"And she never, never stopped loving Jonah. That was the day I finally accepted that she hadn't loved me at all. So many lies. So much unhappiness. From everything I've seen and read about you, it appears you have a good life. The whole state, my state that I've worked to serve all my life, appreciates all you've done for our people." A second later, the man's head drooped, and he was sound asleep.

Jake knuckled his eyes and turned to leave. Alex had unlocked the door and was holding it open. They let themselves out, but not before Zeke commented on the one-of-a-kind marble staircase that held absolutely no interest for either Jake or Alex.

"Anyone feel like talking?" Zeke asked.

"I'm talked out," Alex said, climbing into the backseat of his own car so Zeke could drive.

"I need to think," was all Jake could come up with.

"Next stop, the Sizzler, boys," Zeke said.

Jake's emotions were all over the map on the ride to the Sizzler, where he picked up his truck. He didn't know what he felt when Alex wrapped his arms around him in the parking lot and said, "It's going to be okay, Jake. I just feel it."

Zeke clapped Jake on the shoulder, then looked him in the eye. "This ain't the end of the road, son. You need to think of it as going around a bend with miles and miles of highway still to be traveled. Don't you go doing nothing stupid, you hear me? I don't want you making me ashamed of you. You listening to me, Jake?"

"I always listen to you, Zeke. You know that. I'm going to the SPCA now to get a dog. Call me when you want to hang out."

Zeke cackled. "Well now, that might not be for a while, son. Miss Sophia and I have a—"

"Say what?" Alex roared.

"Settle down, young'un. Your mama has a right to pick her friends, and she told me straight to this ugly face of mine that she could see in my eyes I was a good man. That means good enough for her. You got any more to say, you take it up with your mama. See ya, boys." With that, he walked to his truck and drove off.

"Your mother can't do any better than Zeke,

Alex. Just so you know. Can't you just be happy for your mother if that's what *she* wants?"

Alex clapped Jake on the back the way he'd seen Zeke do. "I was just jerking his chain and talking to hear myself. I like the old guy, I really do. I've wanted Mom to find someone for years, but she was too busy looking after me. She said I had to come first, no matter what. The SPCA, huh?"

"Yeah, come by later and see my new roommate."

"I'll do that. How about I bring some Chinese? You like Chinese beer?"

"How about some sweet tea instead. I think I've had enough beer to last me a good long time."

"Gotcha. Seven okay?"

"Seven's good."

"I still feel like you're my brother, Jake. For whatever that's worth."

Jake grinned. "Funny you should say that. I was just thinking the same thing."

"Go on, get out of here and save some dog that needs saving."

Jake did just that, stopping once at a local gas station to ask where the SPCA was. He took a long moment to wonder why he didn't already know that. Whatever . . .

He got lost twice but finally pulled into a gravel parking area, where he could hear the sounds of dogs barking. He got out and walked over to a fence against which a group of dogs were slamming their bodies. One lone dog hung back, skinny, with big, sad eyes. Jake could count the dog's ribs. It looked tired. As tired and as sad as he felt. He stood a moment longer, watching her, before he walked into the small, cramped, outer office. A long discussion followed, and thirty-five minutes later, Jake walked out with the skinny dog in his arms. As he walked to his truck and opened the door to climb in, he held her close because she was shaking so badly. He crooned to her the way his mother used to croon to him when he was crying and upset over something. She calmed down slowly, just as they reached a vet's office on Old Trolley Road. He knew the vet, Donny Gamble—he'd gone to school with him.

"Do whatever you need to do for her—all the shots, the microchip, a bath, clip her nails. And perfume her up a little; she smells pretty bad. Her name is Lucy Red. I'll wait in the waiting room, okay?"

That's when Jake saw Fancy Dancer, sitting off to the side by an enormous fish tank. She was crying.

"Fancy? What are you doing here? Is one of the animals sick?"

"Jake! I'm sitting here trying to get up the nerve to . . . to put Jethroe down. A huge tree limb fell on him, and his back end . . . I don't have the money to pay for the operation." She started to wail then and couldn't stop.

Jake sat down next to her and pulled her close. She was shaking the way Lucy Red had been shaking. He crooned to her, whispering all kinds of things that later he couldn't remember. What he did remember saying was that he would pay for the operation because little Charlie loved Jethroe. "Wait here, Fancy. I'll take care of this."

Jake ran down the hall, shouting Donny's name. "Damn, Jake, people can hear you in the next county. It's only been five minutes."

"No no, it's Jethroe. I'll pay for the operation. Do what you have to do. You better do a good job, too."

"I'll get him prepped right away."

"You can save him, can't you?"

"Hey, Jake, does the Pope pray? Go on, get out of here so I can get to work."

Back on the bench by the fish tank, Fancy was holding a wad of sodden tissues. "What did he say?"

"Well, when I asked him if he could save him, he said, 'Does the Pope pray?' I think that was a yes."

"I don't know how to thank you, Jake. What are you doing here, anyway?"

"I went to the SPCA to get a dog. Save a dog, actually. I brought her here to get cleaned up, get her shots, and get microchipped. Her name is Lucy Red, and she's all skin and bones."

"That's a good thing," Fancy said, tears rolling down her cheeks. "It will take me forever to pay you back, just so you know."

"I don't want to be paid back, Fancy. Consider it a donation. I was going to call you in the next few days. I'd like to come back and finish out my . . . sentence. I know, I know, I don't have to do that, but I want to. Consider me a volunteer, and I can go home at night and not put anyone out. Of course, if you don't want me, that's an entirely different matter."

"Oh, we do . . . I do . . . We can use all the help we can get. We got two new children, four-year-old twins. Charlie appointed himself as their big brother. He misses you, Jake. I mean he *really* misses you. When he says his prayers at night, you are at the top of his 'God bless' list."

"No kidding," Jake said, immensely pleased at what he was hearing. "Listen, do you want to go get some early lunch? It's going to be a little while. How about we get a pizza at Alex's mom's restaurant? We'll come right back here afterward."

"Okay, but I have to call my mother. She was so upset about Jethroe, and it's not good for her to get upset."

While Fancy called home, Jake walked over to the desk, signed a blank check, and told the technician where they were going. He left his cell-phone number in case Donny needed to call him. "We'll be back in about an hour."

The young technician with a fat pigtail hanging down her back smiled and motioned that it was okay to leave.

Jake looked across the room at Fancy, who smiled at him. Suddenly he felt as good as he had the moment he heard the first notes of Miles Davis's "So What."

In his new truck, with Fancy settled in the passenger seat, the first words out of Jake's mouth were, "Do you like jazz?"

Fancy burst out laughing. "Does the Pope pray? Of course. I love jazz. Do you?"

"One of my true loves." Jake grinned.

Chapter 12

Jake was five days into his new life with Lucy Red. He took his responsibilities so seriously, Zeke and Alex could only gawk and listen in amazement. Cooking special food for a dog. Amazing. Exercising with the dog twice a day. Interesting. Sleeping with the bony creature with the sad eyes. Heartwarming. The house had become a glorified doghouse catering to the four-legged creature. Beyond amazing, interesting, and heartwarming. The best part, though, both men agreed, was that the haunted look was gone from Jake's eyes. And they agreed that Jake was a happy camper.

Jake was ladling out Lucy Red's lunch when the phone rang. He set the bowl that said LUCY RED on it, a gift from Fancy Dancer, on the floor and picked up the phone. It was his friend, the vet, Donny Gamble. He listened.

"I can leave now and come and pick up Jethroe. I agree with you that it wouldn't be wise to send him back to Fancy's until he's fully recovered . . . Of course I can handle the harness and get him out and about . . . Lucy Red could use some company . . . Maybe he doesn't like being in the clinic. I didn't know dogs could get depressed. Do you have a pill for that? . . . I have an idea, Donny. There's a little boy out at Fancy's who is very attached to Jethroe and he to Charlie. It's the weekend, so I can take a ride out there, pick up Charlie, and bring him here so Jethroe can see him. Fancy called me yesterday and said Charlie was in a funk over the dog. Let's give it a shot . . . Look, I can keep him as long as necessary, and now that I'm such an authority on all things pertaining to dogs, you don't have to worry about a thing. Do I owe you any more money? . . . No? Okay, I'll pick up Charlie when the kids' lessons end, and swing by for Jethroe. Three-ish."

Lucy Red nosed her bowl toward the sink to show she was finished. She looked up at Jake, then sat back on her haunches as she waited for him to get the leash. Jake obliged, and man and dog walked around the block three times. Back at the house, Jake handed over a dog treat, and Lucy Red carried it to the pink polka-dotted dog bed that a salesgirl had talked Jake into buying. There were dog beds in every room in the house. Girly beds. Alex had guffawed when he saw them. Bushels of toys that squeaked and whistled were everywhere. By the end of the day, Jake's back hurt from bending down to clean up and store the plush toys in the purple laundry baskets that were also in every room in the house.

The bottom line was that Jake St. Cloud loved Lucy Red more than he'd ever loved anyone, except possibly his mother. The hours until it was time to head out to Fancy's loomed ahead of him. He looked around to get his bearings, opened the refrigerator, and took stock of the ingredients. He could mix up a meat loaf, cook some vegetables, and have it all ready for when he brought Jethroe back. It bothered him that Donny Gamble had said Jethroe wasn't eating.

First things first. Put on some music. Call Fancy and ask about bringing Charlie out to his house, explain about Jethroe and his harness and the wheels that would enable the yellow Lab to get around while he healed. Then he could make his meat loaf. Or two or three.

Jake wondered what it would be like to have a little person, namely Charlie, underfoot in the house. He hadn't been at Fancy's long enough to form any real bonds with the kids or the animals, but he had interacted with Charlie. The little boy seemed to like him, and he liked Charlie, too. He grinned when he remembered Fancy telling him that he, Jake, was at the top of Charlie's "God bless" list at night.

Fancy Dancer. Jake squeezed his eyes shut as he remembered the feel of her in his arms at the vet's. She'd smelled sweet, flowery, and oh-so comfortable in his arms. Like she was meant to be there. Suddenly, he felt warm all over as he wondered what it would be like to take Fancy out to dinner, then maybe go for a walk afterward, where they would stroll along, holding hands. Then, at the end of the evening, a kiss at her door. At which point he'd probably go home and take a cold shower, with Lucy Red poking her nose in the shower door wondering what was going on at that hour of the night.

Lucy Red had become a creature of habit these last five days and had his routine down pat. Lucy Red did not like curveballs thrown at her. That's when Jake realized he was going to have to find a dog sitter if he wanted to have any kind of social life. A dog sitter he could trust. Where did one find a dog sitter? Did employment agencies have dog sitters? Of course he'd want to interview whomever they recommended. He couldn't hire just anyone, not for Lucy Red. He'd want them bonded, that was for sure. Well, he could think about that later. At the moment, he had to call Fancy; and then he had to make a couple of meat loaves for the dogs. Dogs as in plural. Charlie, too. Jeez, what if Charlie didn't like meat loaf? Chicken nuggets. Didn't all kids like chicken nuggets? He thought he'd seen that on TV not too long ago. Just to be on the safe side, he'd pick some up on the way home from the vet's.

Off in the next room, Jake heard a series of squeaks and squeals as Lucy Red played with her toys. He dialed Fancy's number, relayed the gist of Donny Gamble's phone call, and waited for her reaction.

"I'm more than okay with all of that, Jake, if you're willing to help me out yet again. As for Charlie, he'll go over the moon when I tell him. And of course you can keep Charlie for the weekend. I'll pack his things. If it's crucial to Jethroe's recovery, I can have Charlie's teacher make up a lesson plan for next week and even two weeks if you think it's necessary. Charlie's a quick learner and is doing extremely well in school. In fact, he's way ahead of the rest of the kids his age. You realize, though, that you will have to sit with him and help out."

"Sure, no problem. What does he eat?"

"Anything, Jake. We aren't fancy here, no pun intended. The kids eat what's put in front of them. We serve nourishing food, and they all get vitamins. I'll pack some for Charlie."

"Does he like meat loaf?"

"Are you kidding? Charlie loves meat loaf."

Jake's fist shot in the air. "Okay, then, I'll be out around three. By the way, when and if I can find a reliable babysitter as well as a dog sitter, would you consider having dinner with me one night next week?"

"I'd like that very much, Jake. Nowhere fancy, though—again, no pun intended. I just don't have any fancy duds. Again, no pun intended."

Jake's fist shot in the air once again. "I know just the place—jeans, sneakers, and T-shirts and we'll look like everyone else, and I hear the food is amazing."

"Then I'm your girl."

I'm your girl. Jake loved the sound of those words. "Okay, I'll see you in a little while. You're sure now that Charlie will be okay coming here?"

"As long as Jethroe and Mr. Jake are there, he's going to love it and feel pretty special at the same time. Guaranteed."

"Okay, then, I guess we're good to go unless there's anything else about Charlie you think I should know."

The hesitation Jake sensed from the other end of the line brought a frown to his face. He suddenly felt anxious.

"Well, there *is* one thing. Charlie is obsessed with finding a grandmother. He doesn't have one, and he desperately wants one. He has a picture in his mind of a grandmother and . . . we simply haven't been able to come up with a volunteer who meets his requirements. It's all he talks about and prays for before he goes to bed at night. He is convinced she's searching for him and just hasn't found him yet. I've had one of our volunteer therapists talk to him at length, many times, and the little guy is as stubborn as they come. The bottom line is he wants a grandmother. Period."

Jake felt out of his depth. He knew as much about grandmothers as he did about dogs and kids. "I assume at some point there must have been a grandmother in his life."

"That's just it—there wasn't. At least not that we've been able to find in our searches. Charlie's parents were killed in a car crash during a really bad rainstorm. Charlie was home with a sitter, and he was only two. He doesn't remember his parents at all. His mother was adopted, from what we know, and we have absolutely no information on the father at all. It's almost like he hatched from an egg. We did try, Jake, but our resources are limited. Anyway, if Charlie brings it up, just do your best."

They spoke for a few more minutes about nothing important.

There was a smile a mile wide on Jake's face when he ended the call to Fancy Dancer. Yes sir, his world was looking up. The ugly black hole he'd fallen into after his visit to Clement Trousoux had, somehow, magically spit him back out. He could think clearly again, and he gave all the credit to Lucy Red, Alex, and Zeke. He knew in his gut he'd still be in that ugly black hole if it weren't for the three of them. And now, something even better was happening—he was going to take Fancy Dancer out on a casual date. Who knew what would come of that?

Jake shifted into what he called his neutral zone as he started to mix up the meat loaf. Half his mind was on the music he was hearing, the other half on Fancy, Charlie, and the dogs and finding someone who fit Charlie's definition of a grandmother. He was in a good place mentally, and he knew it, reveled in it.

"Mr. Jake, is it true that I'm coming to stay with you for a little while? Where did your hair go? Jethroe isn't an angel, is he? I can carry my books; you don't have to help me. I like meat loaf."

"Whoa there, big guy! One question at a time," Jake said as he tossed a battered green duffel bag with Jake's clothes and the other duffel bag with his schoolbooks into the backseat of his new truck. "Yes, Miss Fancy said you can stay with me for a little while, but you still have to do your schoolwork every day. I had to shave my hair off because it smelled bad from the oil. It's starting to grow back in. Before you know it, I'll have as much hair as you do. No, Jethroe is not an angel. He's missing you a lot. We're going to pick him up right now. I need you to help me take care of him. And I am more than happy that you like meat loaf."

Jake settled Charlie in the passenger seat, made sure his seat belt was buckled, and turned around and smashed right up against Fancy.

"Oops. You really are light on your feet, aren't you? I didn't hear you make a sound."

Fancy laughed. "Charlie has a way of taking over a situation. Thanks again for doing this, Jake. My mother and I both appreciate it. Call me after you get Jethroe home and let me know how he is."

"I will do that," Jake said, feeling slightly drunk at how close he was standing to Fancy and how sweet she smelled. Like a meadow full of flowers on a warm summer day. He shuffled his feet. Fancy shuffled her feet and was the first to step back so Jake could walk around to the driver's side of the truck.

"Mind your manners, Charlie. Make sure you do all your homework, and do not forget to brush your teeth. Give Jethroe a hug for me and tell him we all miss him, okay?"

"Okay, Miss Fancy."

Fancy leaned over and whispered in Charlie's ear. He grinned from ear to ear and gave her a thumbs-up. Fancy laughed out loud and waved as Jake backed up his truck and left the parking lot.

"I bet you want to know what she whispered in my ear, huh, Mr. Jake?"

"Is it a secret? If it's a secret, then you'd better not tell me. Not unless she told you I am the best-looking guy she's ever seen in her life even though I'm bald right now. If she said that, then yeah, I want to know," Jake said, laughing.

"No, she didn't say that, Mr. Jake. Miss Fancy

didn't say it was a secret. If it's not a secret, should I tell you?"

"What do you think, Charlie? Do you think it's something Miss Fancy would want me to know?"

Jake thought he could see the wheels spinning inside the little boy's head as he contemplated how best to answer the question. Finally he said, "Miss Fancy said to be sure to tell you I like your meat loaf."

Jake roared with laughter as he tousled Charlie's blond curls. "You only have to tell me that if you mean it. I'm not a very good cook, but I'm learning. I can use all the help I can get."

"Do you know how to make raisin cookies?"

"I can't say that I do, Charlie."

"You can go on the computer and ask it. That's what Miss Fancy does. She sees it, then writes it down. Miss Alice, who cooks, said she makes a big mess when she makes cookies."

"Does she now?"

"They're good, too. Miss Fancy used to dance. Did you know that, Mr. Jake? She showed me pictures of her in her costume and her special shoes. Miss Angel was a dancer, too, a long time ago. You have to have good feet to dance. Did you know that, Mr. Jake?"

"Well, yes and no. Aren't you lucky that Miss Fancy is taking care of you now and not dancing?"

"Oh no. Miss Fancy said she wanted to dance more than anything in the whole world. She said God had other plans for her. She cries, Mr. Jake. When no one is around. I seen her with my own eyes crying."

"*Saw* her, Jake. Not *seen*."

"Saw. Okay, I can remember I saw her and not seen her. It's sad when ladies cry, isn't it, Mr. Jake?"

"Very sad," Jake said. "But we aren't going to worry about that right now, Charlie. Right now we are at the vet's office, and I bet old Jethroe is already picking up your scent."

"Can he do that, Mr. Jake?"

Jake didn't know if he could or not, but he said yes anyway. "Okay, buddy, take off your seat belt and let's hit it!"

Charlie was out of the truck and headed for the door at breakneck speed, shouting Jethroe's name at the top of his lungs. As Jake and Charlie entered the office, the technicians came running, Donny Gamble right behind them. "Quick, before that dog kills himself trying to get out here," the vet said, running down the hall, Charlie right behind him.

"Oh, Jethroe!" Charlie said, throwing himself at the big dog, who was trying to lick him to death. "I'm so glad you didn't turn into an angel. I missed you, big boy!"

Donny poked Jake in the ribs. "See, this is what makes it all worthwhile. He's going to be fine. Three weeks in the harness, and he should be good to go. Cute kid."

"Yeah, he is," Jake said, his eyes burning at all the love he was seeing right in front of him.

"Be sure to feed him when you get him home. He's barely eaten a thing the whole time he's been here. Lots of water, too, and give him some supplements. I have everything in a bag out at the desk. You're good to go, Jake. Call me if you need me."

"You bet."

Thirty minutes later, Jake pulled into his driveway just as Alex and Zeke turned the corner and came to a stop at the curb in front of the house. "Ah, we have guests and in the nick of time," Jake said as he pondered the best way to get Jethroe out of the backseat of his truck. As Jake pondered, Zeke reached in, picked up the dog, and cradled him in his arms. "Open the door, son, and tell me where to put this load of love."

Alex had the door open before Jake could get to it. Lucy Red was barking her head off at the unexpected goings-on. Jethroe let loose with a deep growl, then did some rather fancy yipping that Jake took to mean he'd get to Lucy Red when he was darn good and ready.

"I have everything set up in the family room. Charlie, you stay there with Jethroe until I can get everything ready."

"He needs to eat, Mr. Jake. I can feed him. He likes me to feed him, and he doesn't make a mess, either."

Zeke and Alex watched as Jake bustled around the kitchen, testing his meat loaves to see if they were too warm or too cool. He fixed plates, got out water bowls, then looked for the special bacon treats he kept in good supply for Lucy Red, who was whining at his feet and sticking to him like glue. He bent down, gave her a big hug, and whispered in her ear. She woofed softly and trotted out of the room. "She loves me." Jake grinned at the stupid looks he was seeing on Alex's and Zeke's faces. "You guys wait here; we don't want to traumatize Jethroe. I'm doing this by the book because I know Fancy is going to grade me on my performance."

"Aha," Zeke and Alex said in unison.

"I need to talk to you guys about something, so don't go away," Jake called over his shoulder.

"You giving the dog that *whole* meat loaf?" Alex asked.

"Well, yeah. The vet said Jethroe didn't eat the whole time he was there. He's starving."

"That's gotta be three pounds at least, wouldn't you say, Zeke?" Alex commented.

"At least." Zeke laughed.

Jake took the food to the dogs in the family room, then returned to the kitchen and dusted his hands dramatically. "I think that all went rather well. Jethroe is allowing Lucy Red to eat with him. A match made in heaven."

"What do you want to talk to us about, Jake?" Zeke asked.

"Alex, do you have a grandmother? I never asked."

"I wish. Both my mother's parents died when I was thirteen. Why?"

Jake explained. "I have to find that kid a grandmother. A real one, if he has one on his father's side."

"Hire some private detectives. My partners and I have a couple we use when needed. They're good, and their rates are reasonable," Alex said.

"Okay, okay, get me their names. I never had a grandmother. At least not that I remember. Fancy said Charlie is obsessed with finding his. You guys want something to drink? Coffee or soda?"

"I'll take some coffee," Zeke said. Alex nodded. Jake made coffee.

"Anything going on I should know about?"

"You been watching the local news, son?"

"I haven't had time, to be honest. Why, did something happen I should know about?"

Zeke looked at Alex, who shrugged.

"What? Damn, don't tell me something else is wrong out on the rig."

"No. That's not it. Clement Trousoux passed away in his sleep two nights ago. The funeral— private, family only—was at ten o'clock this morning. There is no family, just the latest trophy wife. The news played it up pretty good, with all his old pals from the senate who are still around. Like the man or not, he did a hell of a lot for this state. I don't know this for sure, but I'm thinking there's one happy man walking around. Meaning, of course, Jonah St. Cloud," Zeke said.

"I don't feel anything. I should feel something, don't you think?" Jake said sadly.

"It wasn't like you *knew* him, Jake. It's like me and my sperm donor. I'm sure if it was him that passed in his sleep, I'd be feeling just the way you are," Alex said.

"Private service? I wonder why?" Jake mused.

"This is just a wild guess on my part, son, but I'd wager it has something to do with Jonah's maybe showing up and making a scene or something along those lines. *Private* means *private*, and Jonah can't do anything to tarnish his name."

"Where's he going to be buried?"

"St. Patrick's, where your mother's family rests. They showed a picture of the family crypt on the news this morning. Black marble, really fancy for a final resting place. They made a point of saying on the news that the vault will have some kind of special locking mechanism. That was one of Senator Trousoux's last wishes. Makes me kind of think that even in death, the man was still afraid of Jonah."

"Guess that's the end of that," Jake said, his eyes burning with unshed tears. "It's not right that there is no one to mourn the man except . . . well, maybe his wife is mourning him, but not the way most people would mourn the passing of a man who tried to atone for his mistake."

"I like that attitude, Jake. I really do," Zeke said, clapping Jake on the back. "So, if we're not needed here, I'm going to head on out. Just so you two galoots know—I'm in love."

Alex laughed. "Can you believe that? My mother told me last night that she fell in love with this guy the minute she set eyes on him. She loves his bald head. Go figure."

Jake smiled because he knew both men sensed he'd slipped a little and was teetering once again at the edge of his own personal black hole.

Charlie saved the day when he barreled into the kitchen to say that Jethroe needed to poop.

"Okay, then, let's get him outside. See ya, guys. Duty calls."

The black hole closed over, and Jake was safe.

Chapter 13

As the days wore on for Jake, Charlie, and the dogs, Jake realized he was not only content, he was actually happy. He had a strict routine, and Charlie thrived on it. Both of them liked mealtimes, when they talked and talked, and each one learned more and more about the other.

Charlie was a bright little boy with a thirst for knowledge. He knew his letters, his numbers, and could read as long as Jake helped out with the hard words. He liked to draw, mostly pictures of the dogs and his memories of the Dancer home. He laughed and giggled like any little boy. Three days into his visit, he had two skinned knees and a shiner, which he wore like a badge of honor, from running into a prickly bush. He refused to sleep in his bed on the second floor, preferring to cuddle with both dogs on a mound of blankets and quilts.

A week into Charlie's visit, Jake also realized that he had probably laughed more in a week than he had all his life. When the little boy would throw his arms around him and hug him, it was all he could do not to swoon in delight.

If there was a sticking point, it was that after school lessons and a few simple chores, Charlie would inevitably get down to *life's questions*, and woe unto him who tried to slough off on the answers. It didn't take long for Jake to figure out that Charlie was a need-to-know kid.

It was that time again—late afternoon, right before dinner. Lessons were done and the dogs walked and played with.

"Are all mothers beautiful, Jake?" That was another thing: after a few days of calling him Mr. Jake, as he had been taught, Charlie dropped the *Mr.*, saying it was an extra word, and he was just Jake.

"I think so. Why do you ask, Charlie?"

"I don't have a mother, so I don't know if she was beautiful. Miss Fancy said she was. She said all mothers are beautiful."

"Didn't you believe her, Charlie?"

"I do, but I saw mothers that don't look like the mothers on television. What does that mean, Jake?"

"Mothers come in all shapes and sizes. I think every child thinks their mother is beautiful."

197

"Was your mother beautiful, Jake?"

"She was. When I was little like you, I thought she was pretty like an angel."

Charlie nodded. "What did your dad look like?"

Oh boy. Lie or not to lie? Gild the lily? Opt for the truth. *The truth will set you free,* his mother used to say. Then again, she didn't know Charlie. "He just looked like a dad. Do you miss not having a mom and dad?"

Charlie thought about it. "No. I want a grandmother. Tell me about your grandmother, Jake."

"I can't, Charlie. I never had one. Well, I guess I did, but I never met her. I never had a grandpa, either, if that's your next question."

"Did that make you sad? Didn't you try to find one?"

"It doesn't work like that, Charlie. You have a grandma and a grandpa because they were your mom and dad's mom and dad. Do you understand that?"

"I guess so, but I still want a grandmother. Miss Fancy said you're really smart, Jake. If you're so smart, can you find me one? I pray every night for a grandmother, but I still don't have one. Do you think my grandmother is looking for me? How will she know I'm here at your house? What if she goes to Miss Fancy's today to find me, and I'm not there?"

Oh boy. "Well, then Miss Fancy would just send her here. I'd open the door, and there she would be."

"That's a pipe dream, right, Jake? Teddy said that wasn't going to happen. He thinks that because he's a year older than me and in first grade, he knows everything."

Oh boy. "No, that's not a pipe dream. It's hope, and it's wishful. It could happen. But, Charlie, you also have to be realistic that it might not happen."

"Well, I'm not giving up, Jake. I know I'm going to find her, or she's going to find me. I know it," Charlie said, his chin jutting out. Stubborn little guy.

"That's a good thing. Not to give up. Tell me what you think a grandmother should look like."

"She has white hair. It's all in a ball on her head. She wears round glasses that sparkle in the sun—you know, Jake, when the sun gets in your eyes. She always smiles. And she wears one of those . . . I forget what you call them. Grandmothers wear them so their dresses don't get messed up."

"An apron?"

"That's what Miss Fancy called it. Grand-mothers make everything better, and they love their kids. They always hug them and pinch their cheeks. They do that because they love them so much. You know what, Jake? Grand-mothers always smell good. You know, like the food they cook. I don't mean like flowers. I wish you had a grandmother."

"You know what, Charlie? I wish I did, too."

"Oh well, when I find mine, I'll share her with you. Will you like that?"

"I will like that a lot, Charlie." Jake looked at the kitchen clock. "It's time for your one hour of television."

Charlie slid off the kitchen chair. "You know what I noticed, Jake?"

Here it comes. "I think Lucy Red is Jethroe's girlfriend. He likes her a lot. I can tell. Can you tell, Jake?"

"I think you're right, Charlie. It's a good thing."

"I think so, too. But I don't want Jethroe to like her more than he likes me. He won't, will he, Jake?"

Oh boy. "Lucy Red is a dog, so they're dog friends. You're Jethroe's special-little-boy friend. You give him his food and his treats, and you walk him. He lets you *and* Lucy Red sleep next to him. That means you're special."

Charlie laughed. He was off and running to the family room, where his favorite cartoon show was about to come on.

Emotionally drained, Jake sat down as he contemplated his newfound wisdom. Being a parent to a kid, or a stand-in parent, had to be the hardest, the toughest job in the world. How did parents manage when they had two, three, or even four or more kids? Just doing what he was doing was kicking his ass, and he wasn't even out of the gate yet.

Jake sipped at his coffee, which he never seemed to be without these days. He needed to get it in gear because tonight was another date with Fancy Dancer. He had to get Charlie's dinner ready, as well as the dogs', so that when Zeke arrived, he wouldn't have anything to do except pay attention to Charlie and the two dogs. He still had to shower, shave, and "pretty up," as Charlie put it. But before he did any of that, he had to call the detectives to see if they were making any progress on locating Charlie's grandparents.

What the hell was taking so long in this high-tech age? Just the thought of his not being able to come through with a grandmother for Charlie made his blood run cold. He had to find her, that's all there was to it. And if that turned out to be impossible, then he was going to have to find a stand-in who would fit the bill for the little guy.

Jake struggled to come to terms with his own dark thoughts in regard to his own parents or lack thereof. How the hell could he expect a little boy to come to terms with something like this when he couldn't do it himself?

The back door opened, and Zeke sailed in like a mini windstorm. He took one look at Jake's face and said, "Talk to me, son."

Jake explained about Charlie's Q&A that followed at the end of each day's lessons. "Look, Zeke, I can't even handle my own parentage issues, so how can I help this little boy? What if I say the wrong thing, steer him down the wrong road? The kid believes everything I tell him. I have to tell you, he is so hung up on finding a grandmother, it's going to be hell if it doesn't work out. I was just about to call the private dicks to see if they've made any progress. By the way, thanks for agreeing to sit with Charlie and the dogs."

"You looking forward to this date, eh? What's this, the fourth or fifth date?"

"Four if you're counting, and I'm counting. Hell, Zeke, I haven't even kissed her yet."

"All in good time, son. It's not wise to rush into things of such a serious nature," Zeke said, tongue in cheek.

"This coming from a man who set eyes on a woman for the first time just days ago and is head over heels in love. Meaning you, Zeke."

"See, son, the difference is, I've been around the romantic block way too many times, so I was just ripe for the right lady at the right time. And smart enough to distinguish love from attraction and lust."

Jake burst out laughing.

Zeke grinned from ear to ear. "Is this where you now tell me if my intentions are less than honorable where Sophia Rosario goes, Alex will kick my sorry ass all the way to the Canadian border?"

"Yep," Jake said, still laughing.

"Well, my intentions are honorable, so let's put that aside now and figure out what we're going to do about young Charlie."

"You ponder it, Zeke. I have to get them all fed and get myself ready for my big date. We're dining at the bistro this evening, just the way we did the first three times. Fancy likes their lobster-stuffed ravioli. I'm kind of partial to it myself. By the way, I thought Alex was sitting tonight. Why the switch?"

Zeke shrugged. "All Sophia said was Alex does something mysterious on Thursday nights. She doesn't know what it is, though. She said everyone deserves to keep at least one secret, and whatever he does on Thursday nights is Alex's secret."

"Hmm. I didn't know he had a secret. Well, that's his business now, isn't it. At least he got you to cover for him; otherwise, I'd be sitting home sucking my thumb right along with Charlie. He is the sweetest kid, Zeke."

"I know. We'll have a good time. He's got a few tricks to teach me."

"Yeah, well, just you don't teach him any of yours. Like playing five-card stud. He's too young for gambling."

"Nah, we play go fish and old maid." Zeke cackled. "Go on now, I can take care of things here. Get yourself cleaned up. Sophia doesn't like unkempt people in her establishment."

"Zeke, call the detectives. The number's on the counter. Tell them to put some muscle behind their efforts."

"Okay, I can do that."

Jake's eyes devoured the beautiful young woman walking down the steps toward where he was waiting. Angelica waved from the doorway. Jake waved back, but his eyes never left Fancy. She was dressed simply, in slacks, a white blouse, and a denim jacket. Her hair hung loosely to her shoulders. If she was wearing makeup, it was hard to tell. In his opinion, she didn't need anything; she was perfect just the way she was. She smiled and slid into the passenger seat. The smile stayed on her face as Jake regaled her with Charlie's latest efforts.

"I'm not hopeful that we're going to come up with a grandmother for Charlie, Fancy."

"As long as we keep trying, and Charlie knows we're trying, he'll be okay. It's something to strive toward. I don't know how to explain it, Jake. It's like it's Charlie's mission in life to find a grandmother. My mission was trying to be a world-famous dancer like my mother, so maybe that's why I understand it. Sometimes missions cannot be fulfilled. Like me with my dancing and you . . . whatever it is you're striving for, Jake."

"That's just it—I don't know what it is. I don't know who my father is, Fancy. Well, actually I do know, but I just found out. Jonah St. Cloud isn't my father. My whole life has been a lie."

"Ooh. Are you sure you want to tell me all this, Jake?"

"Of course. I would have told you sooner, but I couldn't bring myself to talk about it. Alex and Zeke know. And, of course, Alex's mother. My whole life's been one big lie. I don't know how to deal with that. I'm trying. I suppose I should start back at the beginning so you understand fully."

"I'm a good listener, Jake, and I never make judgments."

By the time Jake parked his truck in the bistro's lot, he'd finished recounting the story of his life. He looked at Fancy and saw tears in her eyes. The tears he knew were for him. He felt his insides go to mush as he waited for her to say something.

"The part that is bothering you the most is your mother. Is that what you're having trouble with?" Jake nodded. "Do you hold your memories of her any less dear? Do you love her any less?"

"No."

"Then what's the problem? Your mother was flesh and blood. In other words, human. All humans make mistakes and hopefully learn from them. It's obvious your mother protected you at all costs. You were her reason for living. I'd say she did one heck of a job raising you, and if you're right, she did it without any help from Jonah St. Cloud or Senator Trousoux. You can't fault that."

"I don't have a name, Fancy. I'm not a St. Cloud. Nor do I want to be. I'm not a Trousoux, either. Clement Trousoux died. I should have felt something, but I didn't. I can't claim his name. Nor do I want to. I kind of feel like Charlie does. He wants a grandmother, and I want a name to call my own. It bothers me that I'm nameless."

"You're *choosing* to be nameless, Jake. A DNA test would confirm that you are Clement Trousoux's son. You have every legal right to take his name if you want to. You can even go to court and pick a whole new name if you want to. The choices are yours. They're options, Jake. If you choose not to avail yourself of those choices and options, that's your prerogative, but you can't say you are nameless. Because you aren't. Are you getting my point?"

"Yes, I am getting your point. I'm working on it." Jake slid out of the car, ran around to the side, and opened the door for Fancy. He reached up for her and set her on the ground. He sniffed appreciatively. And then he laughed. "You smell good, but the smells from inside are even better. I'm starved. Let's go."

Arm in arm, the couple strolled into the bistro and were greeted by a smiling Sophia Rosario. "Same table?" she asked with a twinkle in her eye. Jake nodded.

Seated, glasses of the house wine in front of them, Jake found himself shifting into what he called his neutral zone. Meaning, he shelved all his worries and problems so he could give Fancy one hundred percent of his attention. They made small talk, played catch-up since their last meeting, discussed the cold weather that was due to descend on the state, the kids, Fancy's mother's health, and a hundred other things. But Jake wanted to talk about Fancy, to find out who she really was and how she was going to fit into his life. If that was even possible.

Jake blinked. He must have given off some kind of signal that the conversation was going to change because Fancy's hand went up to the scar on her cheek, and she went rigid. He reached across the small table and took her hand. "Don't do that, please. I don't even see it, and neither does anyone else. It defines you, Fancy. It's who you are now. You can't change it. You told me once you could use concealer makeup to cover the scar if you wanted to. And yet, on not one of our dates have you covered it up. That says to me you are finally accepting that scar. Until now. What did I say to make you self-conscious? And why would you feel self-conscious around me, of all people? I spilled my guts to you in the truck. I let you see who I am. Trust me when I tell you there are scars far worse than the one on your face. I'm talking about the scars that can't be seen, and I have many of those."

Fancy tried to smile. "I've tried to let it go, but I can't. My mother gets so upset with me. I get upset with myself. It's not the scar, it's that I'll never dance again. The scar is just a crutch I use to try to make myself feel better. I've had years to get over this, but I just can't let it go. It's just so unfair."

"Nothing in life is fair, Fancy. Didn't you just tell me I had choices and options? Doesn't the same thing apply to you? What makes you so special?"

"I'm not special. I *wanted* to be special. I wanted to be that prima ballerina. Now I'll never know if it was ever possible."

Jake realized he was still holding Fancy's hand. She hadn't pulled away. "You're special to me, Fancy. Actually, you're very special. I wish I was a poet, so I could put it into words. But, hey, I'm just an oilman with calluses on my hands and oil under my fingernails that no amount of scrubbing can get rid of."

"They're nice, strong hands. Hands that have known hard work. I was wrong about you, Jake. I thought you were a rich, wild, hard-drinking playboy. I believed what I read in the papers about you."

"There was a time when all that was true. I had my come-to-Jesus meeting and got back on the right path in the nick of time."

"You make it sound so easy, Jake."

"No, no, no, it is not easy. The soul-searching alone can about do you in. In my case, I had some help from a delicate little yellow butterfly. You have to look your dragon in the eye and swear out loud that you're going to defeat him." He told her the story of his visit to his mother's grave site and the butterfly's appearance, and about going to see Alex for the first time and seeing the butterfly on his windshield. "God works in mysterious ways, Fancy. My mother used to tell me that all the time. So did Zeke. If I hadn't done all those things that day, you and I wouldn't be sitting here right now. I want you to think about that. Ah, here comes our dinner!"

By the time they finished their dessert and coffee, Jake had a plan in mind.

"Fancy, I have an idea. What are you doing tomorrow morning, say ten o'clock?"

"Nothing I can't put off for a little while. Why?"

"Can you meet me somewhere at ten? I'll explain it when we get there, okay? Can you take it on trust?"

Fancy smiled, and Jake felt his heart start to thud in his chest.

"Okay. Where do you want me to meet you?"

Jake told her. "No problem. I'll be there as long as I don't have to get dressed up."

Jake paid the bill and they said good-bye to Sophia, who just smiled and winked at Jake. He winked back.

Life was looking good all of a sudden.

Chapter 14

Jake was forty minutes early to the meeting the following morning. He wanted to give the Symon brothers a heads-up so they didn't collapse with his news when he introduced Fancy Dancer to them, along with his idea. His earlier call to Alex, asking him to meet with all of them, to keep him in the loop, was more than a courtesy.

Jake hopped out of his truck and ran for the entrance to the office building that housed the Symon brothers' law offices. The sky opened up a moment later, and rain fell in swirling sheets. He'd watched the early-morning news, and there had been no mention of rain in the forecast, only colder temperatures. It didn't matter because there was nothing he could do about it, anyway. It was just that he hated rainy days. He took them as a personal affront to whatever it was he had going on for the day. For some reason, it was easier to get things done when the sun was shining.

There was no one in the waiting room. In fact, Jake thought, there had never been anyone in the waiting room the many times he'd visited. The whole place was silent as a tomb. Then a door opened, and one of the brothers came out to welcome him. "Our receptionist is out with the flu, Jacob. Come in, come in. We weren't expecting you, but that doesn't mean we aren't glad to see you." Elroy called out his brother's name, and Estes appeared as if by magic. These old guys were something else, Jake thought. If he could just keep track of who was who, he'd be home free.

"I should have called, but I only got this idea last evening and didn't want to intrude on your private time at home. I hope this isn't inconvenient, Estes."

"It's never inconvenient. We're here to serve you and all of our clients. Now, would you like some coffee and a beignet?"

"Of course. I could hardly wait to get here, knowing you would have some waiting," Jake fibbed. The Symon brothers both beamed. Jake wondered who ate all the beignets since there was never anyone in the waiting room. He took two of the sugary delights, scarfed them down, and gulped at the hot, fragrant, Cajun coffee. Now he could get down to business.

"Remember telling me about that thousand acres of land we needed to do something with?" Jake began. "Well, I know what we can do with it. And the rest of the property, too. Tell me if you can make it work to everyone's tax advantage." He explained about Fancy, her foundation, the kids, the mother's precarious health, and Fancy's own misfortune. Then he talked about Charlie and the grandmother search and his personal feelings for Fancy Dancer.

"I know this is a lot to throw at you all at once, but my brother, who is not actually my brother, will help, I'm sure. I want that renovated barn on the property turned into a dance studio. It's in excellent shape, so it shouldn't take but a month or so to turn it all around with lighting, windows, and whatever else is needed. Even if Fancy cannot dance, she can teach ballet to others.

"The main house, as you've told me more than once, is rock solid, all repairs current, and can house Fancy and the kids until we figure out what to do with all the other buildings. Workshops, classrooms, whatever is needed. Is this doable?"

"But of course it's doable. The tax advantages to you will be glorious. I wish you had thought of this a few years ago. I think it's win-win for everyone, don't you, Estes?"

"I purely do, Elroy, I purely do."

Hearing that, Jake was ecstatic. "Okay, Fancy is probably out in the parking lot, waiting for me. I have to go get her. And then Alex is meeting us shortly. We're good to go then?"

"Yes, Jacob, we are good to go. Your mother would be so proud of you for doing what you're doing."

Jake stopped in his tracks. He turned around. "How do you know that? Or are you just saying that to make me feel good?"

Elroy and Estes huffed and puffed over their credibility being called into question. "Jacob, your mother told us on more than one occasion that when the time came, you would know what to do with the plantation. She expressed the hope that it would be something wonderful, but she knew it would be, because you are such a fine young man. You can't make this stuff up, Jacob," Estes said fretfully, or maybe it was Elroy. In the end, it didn't matter because both men were nodding their heads up and down.

"Okay, that's good enough for me. I'll be right back."

"You might need this," Elroy said, or maybe it was Estes, holding out a huge black umbrella. Jake grabbed it and ran down the steps and out the door. When Fancy saw him she got out of the car and ran to him. He gathered her close like he'd been doing it for years. Even though the umbrella was huge, they both got wet.

"If it weren't so cold, I'd suggest we stomp in the puddles." Jake laughed.

"Let's put that on our list of things to do when the weather warms up."

Now we have a list. Oh, this is looking better and better.

"Listen, when we get into the office, there's a kind of protocol to follow. I can explain it later. First, you eat a beignet, you say how delicious it is, then you drink the Cajun coffee, and it's just as delicious. You thank them for seeing us on such short notice. The rest you just wing. You know, the social conversation. When that's all done, we get down to business."

"Relax, Jake. I got it. I know how to act in public. I got it," she repeated because of the concern she was seeing on his face.

"Okay then, let's do it!"

Thirty minutes later, Fancy was so stunned she was speechless. "But why? You hardly know us, Jake. This is such a massive . . . I'm having trouble comprehending everything you all have said. Yes is my answer."

"The tax people will be so happy," the Symon brothers said in unison.

"I hope so," was all Fancy could say.

Alex took that moment to fly into the room, his arms flapping, water dripping everywhere. A commotion ensued while the Symon brothers scurried for paper towels to clean up the mess. Clearly no business would be conducted until everything was back to the brothers' satisfaction.

Jake decided to get a bead on the protocol

and shoved the beignets under Alex's nose. "Eat! And drink that coffee lickety-split. By the way, where were you last night? I tried calling you till midnight."

His mouth full, Alex said, "None of your business."

"Yeah, well, I'm gonna make it my business. I'm not involving you in any of this if you're going to have secrets. I want full disclosure, and your life damn well better be an open book." To make his point, Jake reached for Alex's tie and dragged him across the room. "Now, where the hell were you?"

"If I tell you, will you keep it a secret?"

"Hell no! I said no secrets, and I meant it!"

"Okay, okay. I was rehearsing with my band. I've been doing it every Thursday night for over fifteen years, since I was sixteen. We're terrible, just so you know."

Jake's head buzzed. "And you needed to keep this a secret . . . why?"

"Because we're terrible. In fifteen years, we haven't gotten one gig. It's just some old friends from high school. Country-western, Jake. Even my mother doesn't know. You're going to blow it for me, aren't you?"

"No. Not even one gig?"

"Not a one. It's not like we advertise or anything," Alex said defensively.

"Okay, I thought it was something . . . you know, nefarious. I can keep your secret. Not even one gig?"

"Just shut the hell up, Jake. You ever tell anyone, and I *will* kill you."

Jake sort-of-kind-of promised with his fingers crossed behind his back. He couldn't wait
to get outside to laugh his ass off.

Twenty minutes later, with the Symon brothers' blessings, everyone was on board, and the
young people were slogging across the parking
lot in the downpour.

The trio stood in the rain by their respective
vehicles and smiled at one another.

"I think this is a turning point for all of us,"
Jake said solemnly. He leaned over and kissed
Fancy while Alex timed them with his digital
watch.

Neither Jake nor Fancy saw or cared when
Alex left the parking lot. Nor did they care that
they were both soaking wet.

"Kiss me again, Jake."

And, of course, he obliged the lady.

From that moment on, time raced by. Halloween came and went, November blew in with
a gusty storm that finally gave way to a bitterly
cold December, something pretty much unheard of in Louisiana.

The other thing that was pretty much
unheard of in that particular state was the
emotional condition of Jake St. Cloud, who
professed to be hopelessly, helplessly in love
with Fancy Dancer.

He was standing outside Mulvaney's jewelry store, waiting for his friends to join him to help him pick out an engagement ring for Fancy, which he planned to give her on Christmas Eve under the mistletoe.

"Sappy," Zeke said.

"Romantic," Sophia said dreamily.

"Finally," was all Alex could manage.

An hour later, four sets of eyes—five if you counted the frazzled salesman—peered down at Jake's selection. Jake defended his choice by saying, "Fancy isn't fancy, if you know what I mean. She likes simple things."

"And you call a three-carat emerald cut with two-carat baguettes on each side simple." Zeke guffawed. The salesman groaned and rolled his eyes.

"I think what Zeke is trying to say is that this two-carat round solitaire would probably be more to Fancy's liking," Sophia said sweetly. "I've gotten to know Fancy well over these past few months, and I'm sure I'm right. I, on the other hand, speaking strictly for myself, would love that three-carat emerald-cut stone. Wink, wink, hint, hint."

Zeke flushed a bright, rosy red.

"Mom's never wrong, Jake. You better do what she says, or you'll be bringing it back the day after Christmas," Alex indicated.

"Okay, I'll take it!"

Jake's voice was so jittery, Sophia put her arms around him and whispered, "Trust me,

I'm right on this." Jake nodded the moment he got past how nice it was to be hugged by a mother again.

"Lunch, anyone?" Sophia asked cheerfully. "It's on the house."

When the meal was over at Rosario's Bistro, Zeke asked what the game plan was.

"Well, we're all moved into my mother's old home. Brad, the vet assistant, promised to put the big tree up. He cut down the biggest tree on the property with the help of all the kids, and they're probably decorating it as we speak. Fancy has been decorating for days, inside and out. The place looks like it did when I was a kid. Brings back a lot of memories. A lot," Jake said sadly.

Alex, on his way back from somewhere—probably the kitchen to snitch a cannoli—grabbed Jake by the arm and lifted him to his feet. "C'mere, I want to show you something," he said, dragging Jake toward the front door, where a huge bulletin board held pictures of all the bistro's different customers over the years. He pointed to one, and asked, "What's that look like to you, Jake?"

"An old lady with white hair on top . . . holy shit! A grandmother! Who is it?"

"I have no idea."

"What do you mean, you have no idea? Well, get an idea! Who would know?"

"Mom!" Alex roared.

"Is there a fire? What's wrong with you, Alex? This is a place of business."

"Who is this?" Alex and Jake demanded at the same time, pointing to the grandmotherly person in the picture.

"That's Amy's grandmother. Amy is our day cook. Why? Oh, good Lord. The little boy's grandmother. Oh, oh, oh!"

"Where is she, Mom? Do you think she'd agree to be Charlie's stand-in grandmother?"

"I'm sure she would. All her grandchildren are grown. Amy is the youngest. I'll ask her. Be right back."

Ten minutes later, Sophia was back and giving them a thumbs-up. "Amy said she would bring her grandmother by for dinner this evening, and you guys can work it out. Do you plan on wrapping her up in a big red bow?"

"That's it, we now have a plan," Jake said happily.

They separated then, all of them to go their separate ways. "I'm happy for you, Jake. I mean that sincerely."

"I know you do, Alex. And I'm grateful as hell for your friendship."

"Yeah, me too," Alex said gruffly. "Ah, Jake, I have a question. Look, you don't have to answer it if you don't want to."

"What?"

"When are you going to open that steamer trunk?"

Jake shrugged. "It's in the garage. I think about it from time to time. Someday, I guess."

"Why are you putting it off?"

"I don't know, Alex. It doesn't feel right for some reason. How about I open it on a Thursday night before you let me sit in to hear you and your band?"

"You just put your foot into it, big guy. Today is Thursday. I'll be out at your house at six thirty. Try weaseling out of that now."

"Ha! A deal's a deal."

Promptly at six thirty, Jake ripped off the envelope stuck to the top of the old steamer trunk sitting in his garage. The key was as old and rusty as the lock. But it all still worked.

He and Alex dropped to their knees. It took both of them to hold up the heavy lid. "Hold it, Alex, till I find something to prop it open. This old shovel should do it."

"This is your life, Jake St. Cloud Trousoux. Would you look at that! I think this pretty much covers the phrase *father in absentia.*"

Jake's eyes burned as he stared down at the paper trail of his life from the time he was about five years old. "I guess that a couple of years after he found out about me, he started to collect the things he could. How come I feel like a piece of crap right now, Alex?"

"Maybe because you thought he was something he wasn't. I think the man would have been a wonderful father if he'd been given the chance. Look, Jake, here on the bottom is your christening outfit and your baby shoes. Think about *that.* The only way he could have gotten those things was from your mother. I'm thinking that once she realized how much he cared about you, she wanted him to have them. After all, she had you, and her husband wanted no part of her or you, in any meaningful sense. Don't ever try to figure out a mother's thinking. Not ever. You can't win. Trousoux told us that this trunk was the only thing he was leaving you. Which I take to mean, a part of himself. That's how you have to think of it. Now, when you have kids, you can dude them out in that outfit and pass it on down the line."

"You know, for a lawyer, you're pretty smart."

"Yeah. Okay, enough of this. We need to get going, or we're going to be late. Just so you know, Jake, you are the only one—and I stress, the *only* one—who has ever been invited, okay, you blackmailed me into hearing me and my band play."

The practice session took place in the house of one of the band member's cousins, which was empty because the cousin was deployed to Afghanistan. Jake suffered through the suspicious looks but held steady as he took his seat in a rickety, webbed lawn chair.

Jake tried to smile when he wasn't wincing. His stomach tied itself in knots as Alex sang lustily, accompanied by strange sounds on strange instruments. Jake came to understand why the band's existence was the best-kept secret in the state of Louisiana, maybe the entire Gulf Coast region. He also knew with deep certainty that Alex and the Corn Stalks would never get a gig in this or any other lifetime. They made music that only a mother could love, and even that was probably stretching the truth some.

Epilogue

Jake cracked an eyelid and squinted at the bedside clock: seven twenty. He blinked and squeezed his eyes shut. He supposed he could go back to sleep for a half hour, but it was Christmas Eve. *The day.* That night, before midnight, he was going to offer Fancy the engagement ring and ask her to marry him.

Jake bolted out of the bed, his eyes wild. He danced around in the cool air of the bedroom before he cranked up the heat and headed for the shower. Engaged. Married. A lifetime of commitment. *Oh man, this is serious stuff. I hope I'm ready for it. I feel like I am. But am I?*

Christmas Eve. One of the nicest, the happiest days of his boyhood. As he brushed his teeth, Jake let his memory stroll back in time to other Christmas Eves with his mother, who, if he remembered correctly, had always been as excited as he was. Or maybe she just pretended to be excited for the benefit of a little boy. And yet, he remembered how sad her eyes always were on Christmas morning. He remembered the Christmas when he was ten years old—and he knew he was ten because he'd gotten a gift that said it was for ten-year-olds—and it was the year he stopped believing that the guy in the bright red suit could fit in their chimney. Still, for his mother's benefit, he pretended to believe.

He'd gotten a lot of presents, but his mother had only three: one of his homemade jobs, a jewelry box made with Popsicle sticks and glitter; a silk scarf from the household staff; and a beautiful calla lily from Mika, with a big red bow on the pot. There was nothing under the tree from Jonah St. Cloud for his wife. Nor were there any presents for Jonah under the tree, maybe because Jonah was in South America that year—which was a crock, anyway, because Jonah was always somewhere else during the holidays.

Later, when they were cleaning up all the pretty paper, he'd asked his mother why she looked so sad and if she wished she had more presents to open. He'd asked point-blank why Jonah never left her a present under the tree. Her response had been, "Oh, honey, I have everything there is to have, and I don't need anything. Don't you think it's better for someone else to get more presents? Besides, I have you. I don't need anything else." He'd accepted her explanation at the time, but he also realized that the explanation didn't ring true.

Today, he had to go out to the cemetery and pay his respects on the most joyous day of the year. Most people thought of Christmas as the most joyous day, but for him, it had always been Christmas Eve. Yesterday, he had about cleaned out a local florist's supply of poinsettias, his mother's favorite Christmas flower.

His plan for the day was to finish putting together all the bikes and wagons that generous shop owners had donated for Fancy's kids, supplemented by those he had bought so that all the kids would get one. Zeke and Alex promised to come by at nine to help. Then, tonight, after dark, they would take them all out to the house and leave them on the veranda.

Jake shaved, showered, dressed, and was downstairs in twenty minutes. He was surprised to see Alex and Zeke already in the kitchen. He really should think about locking his doors at night.

"We brought breakfast," Alex said, pointing to the egg-and-sausage sandwiches and the Big Boy cups of coffee. "I know we're early, but you said you wanted to go out to the cemetery, and Mom warned us to be on time for our Christmas Eve brunch. She hates it when anyone is late. She's closing down promptly at noon, the only day of the year that she closes early. And, of course, we're closed tomorrow. Just as a reminder, Jake, Amy's grandmother, whose name is Bertie, will be there for what Mom calls a dress rehearsal for tomorrow morning. Mom said she's excited."

"I'm excited just thinking about it. I can't get over how generous all the stores were this year, what with the economy being so bad and all," Jake said, gulping at the hot coffee.

"Mom says Christmas brings out the best in people. You know she's always right." Alex laughed as he reached for a doughnut.

"Jake, if you want to head out to the cemetery now, it's okay with us," Zeke said. "We can do the bikes and wagons. I saw when we came through the garage that you assembled quite a few of them last night. We can handle it."

"You sure you don't mind?"

"Nah. And we put all those poinsettias in the back of your truck and put a tarp over them. All you have to do is get in the truck and head on out. Dress warm—it's cold, and it's gonna rain before long. Sleet more than likely."

"You guys sure?"

"What? Something's wrong with your hearing, Jake? Go already."

Jake grabbed his jacket from the coatrack by the door and left. He was stunned at the amount of traffic on the road as he maneuvered his truck down the busy highway. It took him almost an hour to get to the cemetery, when it should have taken him, at most, twenty minutes.

At the cemetery, he parked his truck, amazed at how many people were there visiting their loved ones. He was shocked when he saw Jonah St. Cloud sitting on the bench Jake and Mika had built so many years ago. But it was not the day to rail at the man sitting there shivering in the cold.

"Need a hand with those flowers, Jake?"

"Yeah, Jonah, I could use a hand."

"You buy out the flower shop?"

"I did. Did you bring anything?"

"No. Be kind of hypocritical of me if I did, don't you think?"

"Yeah, guess so. Why change your stripes now?"

"That's what I thought, so I didn't do it. Sure is a lot of flowers."

"Some of them are for Clement Trousoux."

"Kind of figured that out on my own, Jake."

"Why are you here, Jonah?"

"The truth is, Jake, I don't know. I woke up this morning and knew I had to come here. That's the best answer I can come up with. I've always wondered if the dead know when someone comes to visit. I was never religious, so I thought I'd come out here and see if there was a sign for me. I've been here since six o'clock, and there hasn't been any kind of sign, so I guess I answered my own question."

"You're wrong, you know." Jake told him about the yellow butterfly he'd seen the last time he'd been there and how he'd also seen the butterfly when he found Alex. He half expected his father to laugh out loud, but he didn't.

Jonah got up. "Thanks for telling me that, Jake. Well, I'll leave you now as I'm sure you have a few things you want to say in private to your mother. Merry Christmas, Jake."

"Jonah, hold on a minute. Would it kill you to go and see Alex? Are you man enough to try to make amends?"

"I've thought about it, I really have. The kid would probably kick my ass six ways to Sunday if I showed up at his door."

"Then why don't you try *my* door. He's in the garage, assembling some stuff for the kids for Christmas. If he does deck you, which you most assuredly deserve, he's the kind of guy who will hold out his hand to pull you to your feet. 'Tis the season of miracles, you know. It's never too late, Jonah."

Jonah nodded and walked away.

"Well, Mom, I think that went rather well. I'll be back to let you know if he follows through."

Jake leaned back on the old bench and talked and talked, then talked some more. He was breathless when he finally wound down. He looked down to see if the poinsettias were placed just right. He almost missed the yellow butterfly nestled in the colorful leaves. He grinned then from ear to ear, his fist shooting high in the air.

Still grinning, Jake picked up the three pots of flowers he'd set aside and carried them across the cemetery to the Trousoux plot and set them down. "Merry Christmas, Mr. Trousoux."

Jake sprinted for his truck. Inside, he cranked up the heater and waited for the truck to warm up before leaving. He felt so good, he started singing "Jingle Bells" at the top of his lungs. He was so off-key it was laughable. At that moment, he'd qualify as a singer for Alex and the Corn Stalks.

Damn, he felt good.

As in really good.

Jake pulled out his cell phone and called Fancy. "I just wanted to call you and wish you a Merry Christmas and to tell you that I love you with all my heart."

"I love you with all my heart, too, Jake."

Jake ended the call and turned off his phone. There was nothing more to say. Other than, "Thank you, God."

When Jake pulled into his driveway, he was surprised to see that Alex's car was gone. Zeke's truck was still parked in the driveway. The garage was full of bikes, wagons, and all the things that had been assembled. It looked to him like everything was ready to go. He called out to Zeke.

"In the kitchen," came the response. "Guess you want to know where Alex is, huh?"

"I already know. He went off with his father someplace, probably for coffee. Did he punch out Jonah's lights?"

"Oh yeah," Zeke drawled. "Then, son of a

gun, if he didn't reach out to pull that man to his feet. I gotta tell you, Jake, that boy is not shy. I learned a whole new language in five minutes. I didn't know anyone could talk that fast and say so much in so short a time. I'm not sure about this, but I think we need not mention it unless Alex brings it up."

"No problem."

"How'd you know, Jake?"

"Jonah was at the cemetery. One thing led to another, then another. Just a wild guess on my part. So, we're good to go here?"

"Son, we are good to go. You need to get dressed."

"What's wrong with what I'm wearing? It's cold out there."

"Sophia likes people to be spruced up. Spruced up means white shirt, tie, suit, polished shoes. I'm going home now to dude up. Don't you go shaming me now, Jake. You look your best for this little party. You hear me?"

"No one told me it was dress-up."

"I just did. Sophia said you can bring Lucy Red."

"I would, but she's out at the farm. Charlie wanted her to stay, so I left her. With all the stuff we have to do and the back-and-forth, I thought it was a good idea."

"See ya, son."

"Hey, wait a minute, Zeke. How'd you feel when Jonah showed up?"

"You know what, Jake? He's just someone I used to know. I'll tell Sophia about it later on.

Make sure you smell good when you get to the restaurant, because today is beyond special."

Jake ran upstairs to change into a suit. He was dressed in fifteen minutes and, as per Zeke's instructions, smelling good. All the while he was getting dressed he wondered how Alex and Jonah were doing. Were they making peace? Was it even possible to make peace with all that had gone down over the years? He simply didn't know. Well, he couldn't worry about that any longer. He'd done what he could, and for all he knew, Alex would punch out his lights for interfering in his life.

Jake parked his car in the restaurant parking lot, which was almost empty. The CLOSED sign hung on the front door, and the bamboo shades were down over all the windows. It might as well have screamed *private party*. Jake felt honored to be included in the private luncheon, or whatever it turned out to be. Fancy had been invited but had to decline, and Sophia said she understood.

Jake scanned the parked cars. He didn't see Alex's car anywhere. *Oh shit.* The party was due to start in approximately ten minutes. He did see Zeke's truck and the Saturn that Sophia drove.

Amy, Sophia's day cook, opened the door to admit Jake, then quickly closed and locked it behind him. "Everyone is in the dining room, Jake. Go on in."

"Is Alex here?"

"Yes, he's in the back with his mother."

Jake frowned as he trotted through the restaurant to what Sophia and Alex called the special party room. He could see at a glance that a lot of time and effort had gone into decorating the room for the holidays. A live Christmas tree stood in the corner and gave off the heady aroma all Christmas trees did. There were real balsam wreaths, with red satin bows, on all the windows. The tablecloths were red, and there were silver-colored napkins. Piles of presents, all exquisitely wrapped, were under the tree.

Jake was greeted with warm hugs and kisses to both his cheeks. Everyone chattered and smiled and welcomed him into the very private circle. The only word Jake could come up with was *blessed*. He was blessed.

The menu was simple. Lasagna, summer salad, and garlic twists. And for dessert, eggnog and cannoli, all served buffet style. He could hardly wait to dig in.

Jake looked around to see who, if anyone, he knew besides Alex and Zeke: all of the restaurant employees, Alex's law partners, and, of course, the Corn Stalks, aka Alex's school friends. And Bertie, who could have posed for a Norman Rockwell picture of what a grandmother is supposed to look like. He made a mental note to remind Bertie to be sure to pinch Charlie's cheeks. Then again, maybe that was something all grandmothers did, and no reminder would be necessary. Whatever, he would tell her.

At some signal that Jake had missed, the guests started to head to their assigned tables. Jake felt Zeke's hand on his arm. "You're sitting with us, son. Now, behave yourself and mind your manners."

Jake found it hard not to laugh. "Spoken like a true father, Zeke." Zeke preened at the words.

The speeches were short. Sophia thanked all her employees for their hard work and loyalty and handed out bonus checks. Jake just knew that all those loyal, hardworking employees were going to have their socks blown off with the size of their bonuses. Alex had told him just last week of his mother's plan to give very, very generously. That was a good thing.

Zeke got up and started handing out the presents. That took an hour, and then it was time to eat. And eat they did. Afterward, they sang a few Christmas carols, and the party ended.

"The really good thing this year is I hired someone to come in and clean this all up," Sophia said. "But before we all head on out, Jake—Alex and I have a present for you. It goes without saying that should it not be to your liking, we will both understand." Jake felt a small thrill of trepidation as he reached for a flat box wrapped in red foil and adorned with a silver bow. He opened it carefully and did his best not to cry when he read what was on the paper inside. He bit down on his tongue so hard, he thought he tasted his own blood. He looked first at Zeke, who simply nodded. Then he looked at Sophia, whose eyes looked worried, and lastly at Alex, who was biting down on his bottom lip, his eyes wet. He knew he was supposed to say something. The words just wouldn't come, until Zeke kicked him under the table and hissed, "I told you to mind your manners."

"I . . . I accept being adopted into the Rosario family and I agree to be known henceforth as Jacob Rosario. This has got to be the best day of my life. I don't know what else to say, other than thank you." Tears streaming down his cheeks, he hugged his new mother, who was beaming with pleasure, then his new brother, who whispered in his ear, "I love you, Jake. I did the first moment I saw you. I'm proud to be your little brother. But remember this—I can still kick your ass if you get out of line."

"It won't happen." Jonah turned to Zeke and hissed, "Where is it?"

"Under the table right where I said I'd put it."

"I didn't forget my presents." First Jake handed Sophia a small gold box that he had in his pocket. "My mother said every woman needs a strand of pearls. I never saw you wear any, *Mom*, so I got these for you. I don't know if ladies still wear pearls or not."

"They do, they do. How kind and wonderful of you to do this, Jake. I love them. Quick,

Zeke, hook them up." Which he promptly did. "I could never afford real pearls. Thank you so much."

Then Jake reached under the table and pulled out Alex's unwrapped present, but there was a bow on it. Alex reached out to steady himself. "Is this for real, Jake?"

"As real as these adoption papers, bro."

"He signed it for me?"

"Well, not specifically for you, but it is a signed edition, by Willie Nelson himself."

"I'm not even going to ask you where or why you did this for me."

"That's a good thing, Alex. Think Corn Stalks, and maybe this is what you need to make the music better," Jake whispered in his ear. Alex burst out laughing.

At that point, Zeke declared the Christmas party a success and led everyone out of the room to make way for the cleaners, who would set things in order again.

In the parking lot, everyone hugged and kissed, then hugged and kissed some more as they promised to meet up in the morning at Fancy's to see the kids opening their presents.

On the drive home, all Jake could think about was his new name and new family and how good it had felt when Bertie had pinched his cheeks and smiled at him. He now had a family. And, very shortly, he was going to have a new wife and a mother-in-law. From where he was sitting, it just didn't get any better than that.

For a few brief moments, he thought about Alex and Jonah. Whatever had transpired between the two of them must have been okay from Alex's point of view. He would never ask, and if Alex ever felt the need to confide, he'd listen. That's what brothers did.

Damn, I feel good.

Jake felt even better when, just before the stroke of midnight, he slipped the ring on Fancy's finger. His new fiancée kissed him till he thought he would sail right out of his shoes. And then, exhausted with all their efforts on behalf of the kids, they both collapsed on the sofa, the huge Christmas tree winking and twinkling at them as they fell asleep in each other's arms.

Valentine's Day

The huge solarium at Jake's mother's old home was filled to capacity for the nuptials. For the momentous occasion, the wedding of Fancy Dancer and Jake Rosario, Zeke had set up a special penned-off area for all the animals.

Zeke was giving the bride away. Sophia, sporting a three-carat emerald engagement ring, was the matron of honor. Alex Rosario, Jake's brother, was best man. Charlie was the ring bearer, and his new grandmother looked on.

As the wedding party moved outside so the kids could let loose all the balloons they'd been blowing up for days and the elders could toss birdseed, the happy couple smiled and posed for pictures.

Jake waved his hand and shouted for quiet. "My new wife and I would like you all to join us back in the solarium for some music and dancing to be followed by dinner in our courtyard."

Everyone trooped inside, where Jake made still another announcement. "Ladies and gentlemen, I'd like to introduce you to our wedding entertainment. Meet Alex and the Corn Stalks. Hit it, boys!"

And they hit it.

Out of the park.

On their first gig!

After which, Sophia hired them to perform every Friday night at Rosario's Bistro.

Be sure not to miss Fern Michaels'

WISHES FOR CHRISTMAS

Christmas is a time for family and friends to gather and celebrate old bonds . . . and form new ones. New York Times *bestselling author Fern Michaels brings together the beloved heroines from two celebrated series—the Sisterhood and the Godmothers—for a holiday to remember forever . . .*

Throughout the years, the ladies of the Sisterhood have delivered their own style of vigilante justice to those who most deserve it. But this Christmas, instead of finding and punishing bad guys, all Maggie Spritzer wants is to bring a little more joy to the world—and especially to a beloved teacher from her past. And as the Sisters unite to find her, they learn that no holiday treat is as fulfilling as giving to others . . .

It's a lesson that would come as no surprise to Teresa Amelia Loudenberry— "Toots" to all who love her. With a little help from the other Godmothers, Toots is preparing for Charleston's annual holiday showcase of historic homes. Her mansion is festooned with antique ornaments, beautifully arranged by Charleston's most exclusive design firm. But when the Godmothers sense trouble with one of the decorators, they must tackle a mystery and hope for a happy ending . . .

While staying at the Grove Place Inn as a guest of the Sisterhood's Myra Rutledge, Godmother Sophie meets the inn's owner, Holly Noel Simmons. Despite her name, Holly's feeling none too festive around her handsome employee Gannon Montgomery. Gannon blames Holly for his former company's downfall. Yet the holiday season holds surprises for everyone, and the promise of far sweeter Christmases yet to come . . .

When Sisters and Godmothers unite, the result is a warm and wonderful holiday—with a special touch of magic . . .

Turn the page for a special preview!

A Zebra mass-market paperback and e-book on sale November 2015.

Chapter 1

W hat had started out as a simple, run-of-
the-mill luncheon had somehow turned
into a major culinary event sponsored by Maggie Spritzer for her Sisters, known to their
many adoring fans as the Vigilantes.

Normal luncheons with the Sisters were usu-
ally done on the fly and, for the most part,
held in favorite cafés or restaurants. When
Maggie first came up with the idea, it was because she had a serious matter to discuss with
the Sisters. She knew the luncheon would go
into overtime, and at a public eatery, they
would be rushed, hence this luncheon was in
her own home in Georgetown.

It was well known that Maggie was not a cook,
not even a fair to middling one. Oh, to be sure,
she could throw things together and manage

somehow to make the result edible, but she much preferred takeout, which she warmed up and pretended that she'd prepared. She did, however, have one dish that always garnered praise, a broccoli, three-cheese casserole that was beyond delicious. She always served it with a crisp garden salad, warm, tiny, spongy garlic rolls, and a peach cobbler straight out of the supermarket freezer section.

No one ever complained, and there was never enough left to save, so Maggie was confident her luncheon menu would meet with the Sisters' approval.

Maggie took one last look at her dining-room table. She knew she should have used her once-a-year good dishes, but she'd just been too lazy to take them out and wash them, so she had opted for colorful hard plastic plates with an autumn theme. All gold, orange, and rustic brown. Her centerpiece was an arrangement of fall leaves that matched the plastic plates. All in all, she was satisfied. And she also knew the Sisters wouldn't complain even if she served the food on Styrofoam plates, because things like that simply were not important.

The timer in the kitchen went off just as the doorbell rang. Talk about timing. She grinned as she ran to the door with Hero, her cat, right on her heels.

As always, the Sisters oohed and aahed over the delicious aromas as they hugged and squealed over seeing each other.

Coats and jackets were hung up. It was the end of October, and there was a definite chill in the air.

The women all headed for the kitchen and were surprised when Maggie said, "No, we're eating in the dining room today. And guess what? Today we are having fresh apple cider. I picked it up this morning. Someone pour while I get the food on the table."

The moment everyone was seated, Maggie held up her glass and said, "Happy harvest, everyone! Tomorrow is Halloween. And, by the way, I personally carved that pumpkin you all saw on the front stoop. I just love autumn."

The Sisters all toasted Halloween, then sat back and waited, because they all knew Maggie's casserole had to set for ten minutes before it could be scooped onto plates.

"Are we celebrating something today, or is this just a get-together, dear?" Myra asked.

"Both," Maggie responded smartly.

"Well, speaking strictly for myself, I am all ears," Kathryn said as she eyed the golden brown casserole sitting in the center of the table. Everyone knew and teased Kathryn that she had the appetite of a truck driver because she was an overland driver who handled her eighteen-wheeler like the pro she was.

"Me, too." Yoko laughed. "Spit it out, Maggie, or do we have to eat first?"

"Why don't we be devilish today and break Charles's golden rule that we don't talk business while we eat?" Annie suggested. The others hooted that they were in agreement.

"Any reason why you didn't invite the boys?" Nikki asked.

"Well, yeah, this is girls only. I thought we agreed to do that once a month," Maggie said as she toyed with the serving spoon that would scoop up her casserole.

"Okay, I get it. This is that once-a-month social gathering, *plus* some business, right?" Alexis grinned.

"A hint, a clue, something would be nice," Isabelle said as she popped a tiny garlic roll into her mouth. She rolled her eyes at the delectable delight.

"Does whatever you have in mind involve just us girls or the boys at some point?" Nikki asked, the lawyer in her wanting details and facts.

"To be decided," Maggie said, waving the spoon. "It's just an idea. An idea I've had for a long time. With the holidays fast approaching, it always takes over my mind at this time of year, and I simply cannot stop thinking about it."

"What? What?" Annie exploded as Kathryn reached over to take the serving spoon out of Maggie's hand. Reaching for the plates, she put spoon to casserole and filled them.

"The money from my husband's insurance. I tried to give it to Gus's nephew, but he refused to take it. I never spent a dime of it. I couldn't. I want to give it away this Christmas. I want you all to help me. And then I took it one step further and thought, wouldn't it be nice if you all kicked in some money to match it and . . ."

"And what, dear?" Myra asked.

"Make someone's world brighter and happier. Save someone's life. Do something for someone, or more than someone, who otherwise would stay in whatever position they're in at the moment. This year, for some reason, I want . . . no, I *need* to make the angels sing. I want to *hear* them sing. Does that make sense?" Maggie asked fretfully.

"Of course it makes sense. I think it's a wonderful idea. Count me in," Annie said. "Now, you know if you include the boys, the fund would grow substantially higher," she said slyly. The others agreed as they all started to eat.

"Not so fast," Myra said. "Dear," she said, addressing Maggie, "did you forget we have an organization that Abner is in charge of that donates yearly, very generously and very heavily, during the holidays? Any new charity or person is always welcome. I thought we all had agreed to that. Last year alone, we donated—anonymously, of course—over one billion dollars, which we confiscated from that monster, Angus Spyder. So, I'm not quite sure what it is you want us to contribute to, and while I have no problem with that at all, I guess I just don't understand the end result here."

The women stopped eating long enough to stare at Maggie, waiting to see how she would respond.

"I guess I didn't fully explain, because I'm not clear in my own mind. Sometimes late at night, when I can't sleep, I think about my life, my childhood, my family and wonder, as I think most people wonder, if I could do things over, what would I do differently? Is there some wrong in my past life that I never made right, for whatever reason? Just think about that for a minute. I have an instance, and I've never forgotten it. I don't know if money can or will right that situation, but I want to look into it and try. It's not the same as what Abner is doing with Spyder's money and all those other people's money we helped ourselves to. This is *personal.* That's the best way I can explain it to you all. Does it make more sense now?"

"Well, yes, dear, it certainly does," Myra said. "I think you might be on to something. Let's run this up the flagpole. Now that I understand where you're going with this, I think we should include the boys in this."

"I agree," Isabelle said. The others were quick to agree.

"We can't call them now. It's too late," Yoko said. "They'll be miffed that they weren't included in this luncheon."

"Then we'll do a repeat tomorrow at my house," Nikki said. "That's when we'll run it up the flagpole, and they'll never know this was a rehearsal for tomorrow. How about that for sneaky? Do you all agree?"

"What are you going to serve?" Kathryn asked, her mind jumping ahead to the menu.

"How about a little of everything that is take-out?" Nikki laughed.

"Works for me." Alexis giggled.

Not surprisingly, it worked for everyone.

"So, let's get to the dessert, Maggie," Annie said.

The women talked nonstop as they devoured the peach cobbler, the main topic being that memories, for the most part, were a wonderful thing, be they sad or happy.

"How much money are we talking about?" Yoko asked. "The reason I ask is that Harry and I are going to China next month, and that always puts a big dent in our budget."

"It doesn't matter how much, Yoko. If it's fifty dollars, that's fine. If it's two hundred fifty thousand dollars, that's fine, too. The point is it has to be our own personal money, whatever we can afford. Gus's insurance money is just the cherry on top. I'll be putting my own money in, too. It will all go into one fund, and then, when we're ready to distribute it to whoever needs it, we'll vote on it. I think that's fair. If you all want to keep your amounts secret, that's okay, too. We should vote on that tomorrow. In the end, it might not even come down to money. Maybe there is someone out there from our past who needs something other than money. Something we can provide for them that no one else can. That kind of thing."

"I think this is a wonderful idea," Myra said. "I can't wait for tomorrow. Thank you so much, Maggie, for bringing this up. Sometimes I think we forget that it's better to give than to receive. Oh, this is going to be such a wonderful Christmas. The true meaning of it. Truly, truly."

Annie swiped at her eyes. "Myra's right. This is just what we all need. We've been getting complacent. I agree with Myra. I can't wait till tomorrow."

Twelve minutes later, right on schedule, Maggie's kitchen and dining room were back to normal, with just the autumn centerpiece in the middle of the table. A second round of fresh coffee was served as the girls talked nonstop about what was going to transpire the following day.

"It's going to take a lot of research to track down people from our past," Isabelle said.

"And who better to do that than our four intrepid reporters, meaning Ted, Dennis, Maggie, and Espinosa?" Nikki chortled.

"We need a name for this project," Alexis said.

The group threw out names and titles, but it was Yoko who came up with the one they finally agreed to. Bright Star.

The Sisters all clapped, making their newest project official.